Jamie looked down at his somewhat rumpled clothes and sighed. He headed toward the stables and ordered his horse saddled and readied. Then he jumped astride Phaeton and sped away from Marrenfort.

Enniston rose over the hill, and he urged Phaeton into a quick canter. When he reached the front door, he hopped down and took the steps three at a time before pulling the cord to ring the bell. It opened. He caught movement out of the corner of his eye and went instinctively toward it.

And had found Anne.

They stared at one another, then with a cry she started forward as though to embrace him before restraining herself. Without thinking he reached out, pulled her to him, and pressed his lips down on her open mouth.

She sighed and her eyes closed as he kissed her. After a moment they pulled apart, each breathless. Jamie's gaze roved over her face, and he brushed a strand of her hair aside.

"Anne," he whispered.

"Oh, Jamie. You're safe."

"Yes. For now."

The Lady and the Lieutenant

by

Grace Colline

The Lady and the Lieutenant

Cover Art by *The Wild Rose Press, Inc.*

The Wild Rose Press, Inc.
PO Box 708
Adams Basin, NY 14410-0708
Visit us at www.thewildrosepress.com

Publishing History
First Edition, 2023
Trade Paperback ISBN 978-1-5092-4841-4
Digital ISBN 978-1-5092-4842-1

Published in the United States of America

Prologue

The sun shone hot upon the ship bearing down upon them. Sails billowed out as she came at them—a four master to their three. She outgunned them and out-manned them, and they couldn't outrun her.

The war had come to the *H.M.S. Dorchester*.

Lieutenant James T. Hannigan—Jamie to his friends—stood in the shadow of the fo'c'sle. The ocean erupted from the force of the first cannonball hitting it. The ship shuddered, tilting to one side but stayed upright, though Jamie was nearly tossed to his knees. He finished ramming the wad and the bullet into his rifle and lifted it to aim as the other ship turned its side toward them.

A boom and a whistling shattered the air. The deck of the *Dorchester* exploded up and outward. Jamie flew through the air and down into the water, spinning once he hit and losing sense of where he was. The deep cold shocked him, nearly numbing his limbs instantly. Desperately he swam toward the light, his lungs about to burst, when an enormous eruption smashed into him from the direction of the ship.

The concussion burst his eardrum, shooting pain through his head as he scrabbled upward. A loose plank floated by, and he grabbed onto it to rise to the surface. He broke free of the water, breathing in a deep breath, only to cough and gag at the smoke he inhaled. In the haze around him came groans and cries for help. The other ship appeared to have disappeared into the smoke.

A breeze chilled him but moved the smoke away so that he could see. Debris washed around him, bloody pieces of men washing clean in the icy water.

"Hello? Who's there?"

Nobody answered. Through the clearing smoke the other ship turned about and tacked away.

The *Dorchester* burned, and the shattered hull echoed with screams even as it took on water. He started to swim toward it, wanting to help whoever was trapped within, but with a mighty groan the ship sank below the surface. James watched as its masts disappeared beneath the waves and the *H.M.S. Dorchester* was gone leaving nothing but a roiling sea behind it.

He floated in the silence that followed, clinging to the pieces of decking and suddenly aware of the depths waiting to swallow him whole. He shivered in the cold water and spat the salt from his mouth. Desperately he scanned the horizon for any sign of rescue.

There was none.

He floated alone in the vastness of the ocean as the smoke from the burning ship slowly dissipated, lifting higher into the sky as it faded away. Time passed, and the top of his head burned with the intensity of the sun upon it, even while he struggled with the cold from the icy water. His mind drifted and caught on a memory—a beautiful girl with ash blonde hair smiling at him from the back of a horse. Anne! His faltering heart beat harder as he shrugged off the chill to look about for some sort of help.

Then, he caught sight of something upon the

horizon. Was that a ship? He held his breath, watching, as the object came closer until he could see the sails full and pushing the ship toward him.

As soon as it drew close, he yelled for help, fearing the sounds of the sea would drown out his cry. But then he heard an answering call and continued to wave one arm even while clinging with the other to the piece of decking. The ship neared, and he read *Tempest* upon its side. A line splashed into the water nearby and he struck out, fighting the swells to reach it. Then the rough surface met his hands and he gripped it tight as it was pulled upward toward the ladder lowered over the side.

Though his legs were numb from the cold, he managed to climb the side until arms reached over and pulled him aboard. The deck of the ship felt stable and safe. He lay upon it for a second longer than necessary before rising on unsteady legs to take the proffered hand of the captain.

"Welcome aboard…"

"Hannigan. Lieutenant James Hannigan."

"I'm Desmond Coulter, captain of the *Tempest*. It's an honor to have you aboard. Are there any other survivors?"

It hit Jamie hard, suddenly, that he was the only one. He shook his head and looked out over the dispersing wreckage. His throat constricted.

There was no one else.

Chapter One

The afternoon sun slanted in through the front windows, casting long shadows about the sitting room. Lady Anne Debenham turned the page of her book, then listlessly set it aside. She closed her eyes and sighed.

Nothing seemed to interest her when Jamie was gone.

Her home of Enniston lay but a mile from the Hannigan estate. The two families were close, and she had practically grown up with Jamie and his older brother. But now she felt as though half her heart were gone. Jamie was off in his ship, and her mind conjured limitless dangers for him.

A footstep sounded just outside the sitting room, and she turned as her father came in. A little stooped, with silver temples and thinning hair, he looked vaguely around until he caught sight of her.

"Anne! This just came from Marrenfort. It seems young Lord James's ship was blown up by the French. Damn them—in our waters, too. This is what happens when we have a regent instead of a king."

A weight struck her in the chest, and her breath rushed from her lungs in a gasp. Her mouth worked for a moment as she struggled to say something, but no sound came out. Her hand reached out.

"Lord James is the only survivor. Rescued by a

merchant ship—good on them. Stepping in where they should."

Relief washed over her in a warm flood and her breath eased back into her body. He lived! "Tell me, is he badly hurt?"

"Doesn't say, just that he is coming home."

Anne rose precipitously. "Excuse me."

She pushed gently past her father and went upstairs to her room. Tears erupted before the door closed behind her and she sobbed in great, gasping bursts for a few minutes. Slowly, her tears lessened and she dashed them aside with a swipe of her handkerchief. Casting her afternoon dress onto her bed in a heap, she changed into riding clothes and swept downstairs to the servants' door which led to the stables. Once there she collected her mare, and a groom came up as she pulled the saddle off its stand. Anne shouldered past him without relinquishing the saddle and slung it over the gray back.

After securing it, she was up and guiding her horse out of the yard and onto the drive that led away from Enniston. She urged the mare into a canter, and then pushed her faster as she rode hard away from home. Her father's voice echoed over and over in her head, repeating the news that Jamie was alive and tears sprang forth yet again.

She could not remember a time when she did not love Jamie...his quiet, introspective ways—so different from his older brother. The calm manner he sat and rode his horse, the half-smile that played about his lips when he spoke to her...Her heart clenched, then pounded uncomfortably in her chest.

Her horse slowed and she reached down to pat the mare's shoulder as they trod along. The lane lay

5

shrouded in shadow as the sun sank lower in the sky. She looked about, lost for a moment, then recognized a neighboring farm and rode for a while along the narrow road.

She turned down another lane and was about to rein her horse around when a gunshot sounded off to her right. Her horse jumped and shied to the left, then jumped the stone wall and came crashing down on the other side.

Anne tumbled free, bracing herself to hit the ground and rolling away from the horse. She came to a stop next to a tree and used its trunk to steady herself as she stood rather shakily. Her horse had risen to her feet, but was favoring a forefoot.

Anne noted a farmhouse nearby and caught up her horse's reins to lead her there. Her own leg ached from where it had twisted, and she limped along with her horse toward the thatched farmhouse. Once she reached it, she brushed off her skirt and sleeve before knocking on the door.

Just then, a young man bounded out the door holding a little girl of about two in his arms. Behind him, a young woman with a somewhat messy bun, held the child's hand and laughed. Her smile froze when she caught sight of Anne. The young man's eyes flew wide at sight of her.

It was Edwin, Lord Ashton, heir to Marrenfort and Jamie's older brother.

Anne knew him well, and was confused by the context within which they were meeting. But he smiled widely after a moment.

"Lady Anne Debenham, come meet my family."

She advanced slowly, acknowledging the little

curtsey the young woman dropped. "This is my wife Bessie, and our daughter Elsie."

The girl tapped his arm. "We aren't married."

"Yet," he replied.

Anne shook her head. "I don't understand."

"Well, it is as it appears. Bessie and I met and fell in love. Elsie is the result."

"Does your father know?"

Edwin bent and kissed the little head before answering. "No. Bess and I haven't exactly formalized anything yet. Bit tricky with the vicar, and Father isn't going to take it well. Especially with Jamie going to sea."

He looked up, though, and smiled. "We'll clear all of that up one day. Right now, we meet when we can, and I help out when possible. Luckily, I don't have a job like Jamie. And Father doesn't ask too many questions."

"Have you heard about Jamie?"

Edwin frowned and focused on her. "No. What about him?"

"His ship was destroyed by the French."

Edwin's face drained of color, and she added quickly, "Jamie was the only survivor."

He sighed. "Leave it to Jamie to survive something like that. Is he all right?"

She shook her head. "I don't know. The note from your father didn't say. But he is coming home."

Edwin nodded. "Well, that's good, I suppose." He glanced at her again and added, "I hope you can be discreet, Anne…"

"I won't tell your secret, if that's what you are wondering."

"It is. I will tell Father in time…but now…not with this news of Jamie. We must see how he is first."

Anne nodded. Edwin's horse was brought from the stable. He kissed Bessie and Elsie then swung up. Anne was helped up onto her mare and they set off. Nothing but the sound of birds and the deepening shadows met them as they jogged sedately along to the main road.

"Shall we canter?"

Anne shook her head. "Ash was limping earlier…I don't want to push her."

"She seems sound enough, but oh well."

"You needn't stay with me. I will be all right."

"No, this way I can be seen with you and it may cover any absences. Father has been questioning me rather closely. I can say I am riding out with you."

A knot of anger clenched in her chest at being used in such a way, but it dissipated as she considered the magnitude of his secret. Edwin had always been rather self-centered, and now was no time to expect him to change.

They parted ways when they reached the drive to Enniston. Edwin paused for a moment.

Anne hurriedly said, "Please, Edwin, let me know about how Jamie is as soon as you hear. As a friend, I would like to know."

"Of course, Anne. I'll send a note."

She half-smiled and swallowed. "Thank you."

She rode up the rising gravel road toward the hilltop manor house.

****

Hours later, as she readied for bed, a maid brought her a note with Edwin's seal upon it. She quickly broke it open.

He is well. He will be home within a month.
–E

Clutching the note to her chest, Anne curled on her side and pulled the covers up. A sigh of relief burst from her, and she gave herself up to the feeling.

Chapter Two

Jamie woke with a start, sweat dripping from his forehead and a harsh pain shooting through his head. He gasped again, as though the air were not warmed and clean but cold and filled with smoke.

Pushing himself up, he dragged in a deep breath and willed his beating heart to calm. It had been two months since the loss of the ship and his ultimate rescue, and still the dreams plagued him.

Wrestling free of the bedclothes, he stepped out onto the floor, his bare feet recoiling from the cold wood. The little fire had died down, but its warmth still seeped forth, warring with the chill of the night.. He shivered a little, his skin breaking out into gooseflesh as he reached over to pull a shirt on over his head.

Jamie stoked the fire and added more coal to warm the room. His father's house had always seemed colder than it actually was, but he didn't know why all of a sudden, over the past few weeks, he was so prone to break out into cold sweats.

In his mind he heard the crew's dying cries all around him, the dead calling for him to save them. He bent over, pinching the base of his forehead as though he could eradicate them from his mind.

He glanced at the clock, barely lit by the ghostly light of the fire. He rose, moved to the window, and pushed the curtain away. Sunlight glowed along the horizon, casting the sky in green and pink. A clear, cold day dawned.

Slowly he dressed, pulling on his warmest socks, thickest wool jacket, breeches, and his riding boots. He rummaged through a drawer for his gloves, then drew them on as well. Finally, he knotted a scarf around his neck and stepped free of his room.

His boots tapped on the wooden steps, some of which groaned lightly under his weight. He worked his way through the maze of passages to exit through the back of the house, passing servants who stared at him wide-eyed. He ignored everyone.

The cold fog enveloped him as he exited the great house. But sunshine burned down through it and the frost began to melt on the grass. Stone walls rose up from the clearing mist and he pushed through a large wooden door. He made his way to one of the stalls. A bay head bobbed over the door and sniffled amongst his hands.

"Sorry, Phaeton, no treats today."

The stallion nudged his chest and pulled his head back in for a moment, turning his back on Jamie.

"Are you wanting to ride, Lord James?" A groom shambled up.

"Yes, if you don't mind getting him ready."

"Just a moment." He reached up for the halter then entered to capture the big bay and lead him out.

Phaeton swished his magnificent tail and walked steadily along, head up and bobbing about. He was brushed thoroughly then saddled, and finally his bridle put on. Jamie vaulted aloft and took up the reins before guiding his horse out past the paddocks.

The morning shadows spread long across the fields

as he rode, the sun peeking over the tops of the distant hills. Jamie rode along, Phaeton kicking up his heels from time to time. They came to the forest that covered the western side of Marrenfort, his father the Marquess of Marrenfort's estate.

He breathed in the cold air and breathed out white clouds that dissipated. He urged Phaeton into a canter, and they rocked gently along a path with branches arched overhead. The path dipped down to the right where they diverted to the left to avoid Gypsy's Gate—the treacherous crossing point. Instead, they jumped over the stream before continuing up the rise to the Folly.

He reined in his horse and slowed to a walk as they neared the faux Grecian temple. His mother had commissioned it before she died, and his father had ordered it finished after she had passed. The trees had been cleared in front of it to provide an overlook down to the main drive up to the manor. Jamie rode around the side of it, only to come upon a flea-bitten gray horse grazing in front of the temple.

The mare was saddled and bridled, her reins lying on the ground. From the confines of the temple came a startled cry and he leaned down slightly to peer in. A woman in men's riding breeches stood amongst the columns. Her ash blonde hair was pulled up in a loose bun at the back of her head. Tendrils curled around her face and neck. Blue eyes looked out from under expressive eyebrows as she stared at Jamie.

"Lady Anne, what are you doing here?"

"Jamie! You're home!"

He glanced away, then turned back to her. "Yes. For now. Others weren't so lucky."

She bit her lip, but her gaze stayed locked on his. "I know you will never forget what you went through, but we are grateful to have you home safe."

"I don't...what are you doing here?"

Her eyebrows came down as she frowned and said, "I have your father's permission to ride on the estate."

Jamie closed his eyes for a moment and tried again. "I mean, so early in the morning."

"I might ask the same of you..." She tilted her head as she looked at him.

He rubbed a hand over his face and pushed his hair up. "I couldn't sleep."

"Still?" Her sympathetic voice echoed as she bent to pick up her horse's reins.

"Mmmm."

She put a foot in the stirrup, pulled herself up into the saddle, and threw her other leg over the side. Jamie grinned to himself. Anne had always ridden thus around the estate. She could ride sidesaddle as expected when in company, but by herself she preferred to ride this way, and no one had been able to prevail upon her otherwise.

She pulled her horse's head up and gazed at him. "Where are you off to?"

He shrugged. "Just anywhere. What about you?"

She sighed, and her breath condensed before her in the rising sunlight. "I had intended to ride down to the town to visit my mother before Father got home this afternoon."

"Ah." Lady Anne's mother had run off with the steward and the two lived on a small farm on the outskirts of Brumley, the nearby village.

"How is she?"

13

Lady Anne looked down and fiddled with her horse's mane. "She seems fine. I think I am finally getting used to the situation, but I still find I dislike Havers."

"I can understand that."

"I just don't see what he gives her that we didn't."

"I suppose they were in love…"

Anne swept the thought away with an impatient hand. Their horses fell into step together as they rode down toward the path.

Trying a different tack, James asked, "Have you seen my brother recently?"

Anne frowned. "Why does everyone assume I know where Edwin is?"

"Well, where one finds Edwin, one often finds Anne," he replied with a pang of jealousy.

"When we were younger, perhaps. Nothing more than friends."

"Oh, well, it's always good to have friends," he said a little lamely.

"Yes!" She turned to him with an odd expression that vanished after a moment.

They came to a break in the path, one way led to Anne's home, while the other continued on along the stream and down to the little bridge at the main road. Jamie pulled his horse up and looked over at Anne. She gazed back evenly, her face devoid of expression.

"Are you going back to the navy?" she asked as though wishing to prolong the moment.

He shrugged. "I've been reassigned and will be heading out in a couple days. Assigned to the *H.M.S. Waynflete*. Captain St. John Ellis."

She glanced away after a moment and urged the

horse onward. They were some ways up the hill when she tightened her heels and her horse broke into a gallop.

Jamie watched her go, feeling the familiar pull he always felt around Anne. He did not understand it, but wanted to go after her. He shook himself; he had no reason to go to Enniston today or any day for that matter. Everyone knew that Anne and Edwin were a couple. Or were intended to be anyway. The thought saddened him, and he tried to push it away.

Letting Phaeton choose his path and speed, he rode back to the house,. He truly knew the woods and fields around Marrenfort like the back of his hand. He, Edwin, and Anne had ridden and run through every thicket and hedgerow as they had grown. Riding to hounds through these very paths and over the occasional fence was always thrilling, though he hated the ending enough to have decided fiercely never to go again.

Edwin was the eternal sportsman. Hunting, shooting, rowing, he loved it all. And if their father sometimes wished aloud that he would be a bit more serious, Edwin would simply laugh it off. Everyone loved Edwin.

Though an athlete like his brother, James was more serious. Books had taken up much of his childhood, and a propensity to read had stayed with him as he had grown, something his father never understood. His mother had, though, until she had died some years before. In that way, he and Anne understood one another. Both had lost their mothers, though in different ways.

He looked up in time to see that Phaeton had brought him home while his mind had wandered. The stables lay up ahead and his horse's head bobbed with each step in anticipation of food and water.

Phaeton made his way into the courtyard of the stables and to his own stall. A young groom ran up to take the bridle as Jamie dropped down. He patted his horse gently before making his way back to the house.

Breakfast was still out, and he helped himself to some sausages, tomatoes, and toast. Someone called a greeting down the hall and his brother breezed into the room.

"Ah, Jamie, out for an early ride I see!"

"Yes, where are you off to?"

"Going up to Enniston to see if Anne wants to ride."

"She was out this morning."

"Well, damn. Maybe I'll take the barouche out then. We can drive down by the lake and watch the sculling."

The old unease struck James as his brother talked, though he was at a loss as to why. Why should it matter if Edwin took Anne for a drive? They'd been riding out for years.

"Can I go along?" he asked without thinking.

Edwin stilled, and for just a moment panic crossed his face. Then it smoothed over and he forked a bite of egg into his mouth. "Maybe not this time, Jamie. You understand?"

Jamie did. But surely Anne would have a chaperone... The thought stopped. Anne was a bit unconventional, and with her mother out of the picture, she seemed to simply write her own rules. His hand clenched. He hissed in pain as the embossed silver handle of the knife bit into his palm.

"Careful there!" Edwin smiled and tossed his napkin down. "Need to call for the barouche." He swept out.

Jamie leaned back and set his own napkin down next to the plate. He was of age, a lieutenant in the navy, which was a respectable career for a second son. Granted, so far it had been disastrous.

Was this what he was going to do with the rest of his life?

A niggling fear disquieted him. Would he be able to even serve on a navy ship, or was his nerve gone?

Suddenly, he wished Anne were there to talk to. Her mere presence calmed him and…

And what?

He stood abruptly, nearly knocking the chair over. Could it be he cared a little too much for Lady Anne Debenham? His mind shot to Edwin. Though taller and broader than his older brother, Edwin had a way with people that he, Jamie, did not have. After all, everyone loved Edwin.

He made his way to his room to change from his riding clothes. His new uniform lay folded on the chair, and he glanced over at it. It would need to join his other clothes in the trunk within the next day or so. He would be on his way to Portsmouth to meet his new captain.

His hands slowed in their buttoning of his waistcoat. Anne? He stilled…

Anne.

The truth hit him hard in the chest and he nearly gasped in pain. He was in love with Anne… What could he do that Edwin could not? Edwin the heir, the golden boy. His brother.

Slowly he sat down on the edge of his bed. His

eyes closed and he let out a long breath. Somehow, he needed to control his feelings until he left for Southampton. But how, when his heart raged in his chest at the thought that she might love his brother?

Jamie stood and paced around the room, thinking. He would master this—he had to!

Chapter Three

Anne guided her horse along the track leading home. The red brick edifice rose from behind the hill and stood on a rise before a long pool. Water lilies floated in the water and a few ducks scooted along the edge. It looked peaceful, and she sighed. It was home.

A groom met her to take her horse and she trudged up to the back entrance where a footman sat smoking. She went past him and into the manor, winding through the maze of rooms and halls until she reached the upper rooms. As she turned the corner, she nearly bumped into her father who seemed to spring up, holding the newspaper before him.

"Father! You're home!"

"Yes, just. Anne. Look here, the Americans have declared war!"

"War? Whatever for?"

"Never liked Americans. Arrogant."

"Yes, Father, but why did they declare war?"

"What?" He looked askance at her, and she pitched her voice louder.

"War. Why?"

He shook his paper and folded it. "Damned Yankees claim we are overstepping our bounds. England rules the seas; they need to get used to it. We stop a ship or two—what of it?"

"The Americans might take offense at that," she

said, but low enough that he did not hear.

He wandered off to his library and Anne sighed as she looked around.

Dissatisfaction reverberated through her, along with a restlessness. All her life she had been simply taken for granted, and now she found herself wishing to break free. Free of her home, of expectations…even of Edwin.

She considered for a moment as she straightened the blooms in a flower arrangement. He had forever tied her to him on the strength of a single secret she had merely happened upon. Her eyes closed and she took a deep breath as her mind went to Jamie.

Anne shook herself. Now was not the time to daydream about impossibilities. Her father would expect her to marry Edwin, though she knew that would not happen. Some other firstborn son, then. Well-born of course. But not Jamie…

No.

With a twist of her hand, she plucked off a rose and stalked out the French door to scatter the petals to the wind. They fluttered about, falling across the grass in a haphazard way that captivated her somehow, like butterflies dying.

Sighing forcefully, she went to the parlor where the piano sat in the corner. With due diligence she began, fingers moving from memory a series of songs that she might be called upon to play when her father entertained the Cathcarts of Leighdon, Wilfords of Sattersby, and more. And of course, the Hannigans of Marrenfort.

Her finger struck an off chord and she paused. Perhaps she could ride over to Marrenfort to see Jamie one last time before he left for the navy. She rose to go change when the bell rang. She went into the main hall and saw Edwin in the foyer.

"Edwin! What are you doing here?"

"Driving past in the barouche and wondered if you'd go for a ride."

Reluctantly, she smiled and said, "Just let me get my pelisse. Shall I pack us a picnic?"

His face lit up at the mention of food and she sent a maid to the kitchen. Trotting quickly, she went to the cloak room where she had left her pelisse and pulled it on, her fingers blurred as they fastened the buttons. She picked up the simple straw bonnet that was there and carefully set it over her hair before tying the ribbons. Then she rejoined him in the foyer and took the arm he offered to her.

Minutes later she was sitting on the seat of the barouche while Edwin drove on the box. "I meant to ask if you'd prefer the box seat."

She shook her head and watched the fields and trees go by. "No, I'm fine down here."

"Good. I prefer to drive unencumbered." He was quiet a moment before saying over his shoulder, "Lucky in a way that you happened upon us. Gives me an excuse to go out—everyone will just think I am courting you and not think twice."

"People already think so..." Her voice trailed off as she thought of Jamie.

"Excellent. Works out well for me, don't you think?"

"And what about me?" she murmured, her voice carried away by the breeze.

They travelled in silence for some ways, turning

onto the main road and then going down to a small country road off to the left. Anne reached down and set her hand on the handle of the basket as Edwin pulled up to the small cottage. Elsie ran out, followed by Bessie whose messy braid was pulled over her shoulder.

"Oh!" Bessie cried. "It's you!"

Edwin hopped down from the box and gathered the little girl quickly into his arms, before bending to kiss Bessie. Anne glanced away as they greeted, then reached out and took the little girl into her arms.

"An-An!" She giggled.

"Yes, I'm An-An!"

"Da!" She swung her arm toward Edwin.

He reached out to tickle her without letting go of the young woman.

"Bessie, how are your family?"

"They are well, Lady Anne, thank you for asking."

"And I can see this little one is doing fine!" She bounced the little girl who laughed and patted her shoulders. "Aren't you, Elsie?"

"An-An!"

"Come along with An-An and we will go for a walk down by the fields." She set Elsie down on the ground and grasped her hand as Bessie and Edwin disappeared into the house.

They meandered along the track beside the hedge. Out in the field a workhorse hitched to a plow plodded along, pulling now and then when the plow stuck. The man on the back of the plow raised a hand and Anne waved back. Little Elsie's hand fluttered as well.

After a time, Elsie began to whine. Anne picked her up and carried her for a while. When they reached the house again, she set her up into the barouche and fed her ham and bread from the basket until Edwin and Bessie reappeared. By then, Elsie had fallen asleep on the seat of the barouche.

Bessie's gaze seemed fixed on her knees and she barely responded to Anne's greeting. Anne handed her a slice of bread with a thick piece of ham on it and the girl nodded her head bashfully before taking a bite. Edwin had piled his slice full of different meats and cheeses and bit off a large chunk, grinning down at Bessie and then over at Anne.

The shadows had lengthened by the time Elsie woke up and they said goodbye. Edwin kissed them both and climbed up onto the box while Anne settled on the seat. He chucked to the horses, and they went off. When Anne glanced backward, Bessie held Elsie on her hip and waved.

They were quiet on the way home, each enveloped in their own thoughts. When they pulled up at Enniston, Anne got out.

"Thank you for the ride, Edwin."

"My pleasure!" He winked.

He drove off, down the winding approach until he disappeared into the woods. She went inside, slowly unbuttoning her pelisse as she climbed the stairs. By the time she reached her room, her maid was there ready to take her pelisse and bonnet. Her dress had gotten stained by small fingers and Everly remarked upon them as she took the dress to be cleaned.

"What 'appened 'ere?"

"I dropped a bit of ham on my lap."

"'Ow many times?" She was still shaking her head as she exited.

Anne drifted to the window, smoothing the skirt of

her lavender afternoon dress. Outside, the late afternoon sun had settled on over the western hills and sank below the horizon.

As she went down the stairs, the butler announced the arrival of the Hannigan brothers and Anne's heart flipped a little when she saw Jamie's face. Edwin appeared behind him, straightening his waistcoat. He'd changed but his hair still fell about his head after being windblown all day. Her gaze returned to Jamie.

"I've always liked that color on you," he said.

She smiled at him, "Well, Lord James, for that you may escort me in to tea."

He grinned and held out his arm for her. She laid her hand gently upon it and they moved to the parlor where the tea cart already sat.

"What are you both doing here?"

"Don't you remember asking us to tea the other day?"

She shook her head. "No, I don't. But perhaps I did…"

"Or perhaps we invited ourselves, imposing on the longstanding friendship."

"Ah. Now that I can believe." The corner of her mouth crooked up at him and was rewarded with his rare, wide smile that crinkled his eyes and warmed her through.

"How was the sculling?" Jamie asked.

Her eyes widened. "The what?"

Edwin quickly intervened. "Sculling—you remember Anne. Out on the lake today."

"Oh, yes, of course. Well, as sculling usually is… How do you take your tea, Edwin?"

"With sugar, one, thank you."

She handed a cup to Jamie, "I know you take yours black."

She was rewarded by another smile. She could feel herself glowing under his gaze and was suddenly shy. Her hand shook a little, handing the small plate of crispy tarts over to him, but she mastered it after a moment.

Her father strode in, sat in an empty chair and reached for the macaroons. She poured his cup, splashing a dollop of cream and two sugars into it before passing it over. He drank deeply and sighed.

"Tea! A true Englishman's drink!" he said loudly.

"Actually, it is from the Orient," said Edwin in a low voice.

"What? What was that?"

"I said you're right, sir."

"Damned right I'm right."

Anne took the plate of macaroons from him and held out the crispy tarts instead. He held up a hand and she set them back down. Talk faltered with the arrival of her father, and she bit her lip thinking of something to say. But Edwin beat her to it.

"What do you think of these Americans, sir?"

"Americans? Americans, you say! Blast them! How dare they declare war on us!"

"Quite right, sir!" said Edwin.

Anne flashed her eyes at him, but he simply grinned at her before turning a serious face on the earl.

Jamie lifted his head. "I can wish it were otherwise. I shall be going into the thick of it."

A cold hand suddenly clutched Anne's heart and she stared down into her cup. The fragments of leaves made a pattern. She wished mightily that she could read it and find that Jamie would be safe.

"Anne?"

Her head shot up and she stared at him, "Yes?"

"What do you think of the French siding with the Americans?"

"Oh…well, it is as I would predict. The French certainly have no love of England."

He gave her the ghost of a smile and she mirrored it, allowing herself to stare into his deep brown eyes for a moment before holding the teapot out for Edwin.

A yelp brought her attention back. Edwin's cup had overflowed onto the Persian rug. She set the teapot down and snatched up a napkin to lay on the spot. Edwin laughed out loud. Anne blushed and her father seemed oblivious.

"Jamie, you would know about the French. Wasn't it a French ship that blew up the *Dorchester*?" Edwin said.

"Yes, yes it was." Jamie glanced down and his voice was low.

"What happened?"

Jamie blanched suddenly and his hand shook. She reached for him, her hand atop his and he looked up into her eyes. She almost gasped at the pain and fear there.

"I am of half a mind to play a song, if you would all indulge me," she said, then rose and went to the piano.

She played a calm, but lively tune, one of the new waltzes, casting a glance at Jamie now and again as he slowly gained control of himself. His gaze was riveted upon her, and she nearly dropped a chord now and then. She finished the song and bowed her head when they clapped. Edwin seemed to take note of the clock suddenly.

"Come, James, we are expected at home. Father will want to take his daily turn about the gardens."

Jamie rose, took her hand and bowed long over it. When he looked up into her eyes, there was gratitude in his. Edwin grabbed her hand free of Jamie's grip and kissed it loudly before pulling his brother after him and out the door.

They climbed onto their horses and cantered off. She could not help but note that Jamie sat his horse better than Edwin—not surprising since he rode so much more often.

Anne leaned against the column that held up the roof over the front doorstep until they had disappeared from sight.

Chapter Four

Jamie rode ahead of Edwin, his anger pushing him faster. He had no doubt his brother had brought up the *Dorchester* so he would falter and show his feelings before Anne. How he had divined Jamie's feelings for her, he didn't know. But one look from him had been enough to tell him it was so.

He turned his horse to avoid Gypsy's Gate and they galloped down the little ravine instead. Phaeton chose to charge straight up the rise rather than take it at an angle. Jamie could hear Edwin behind him and out of the corner of his eye saw him take the gate. He turned to yell, but Edwin's horse had already cleared it, albeit barely and came down hard on the other side.

Jamie pulled his horse up and blocked Edwin's way. "What do you think you're doing?"

"I'm riding, just like you."

"You are taking chances!"

"You mean the gate? I've taken it before. Jasper can handle it."

"You have responsibilities. You shouldn't jump things like that."

Edwin maneuvered Jasper around and went past Jamie. "I'll thank you to mind your own business, James. I know what I can handle."

He rode off over the hill toward Marrenfort. Jamie urged Phaeton forward into a steady walk to arrive at the stable well behind his brother. He didn't understand his brother's mercurial moods. He could go from happy-go-lucky, to somber to angry in an instant. Looking up toward the stable where his brother was walking off toward the manor, he urged Phaeton into a trot up to the large wooden doors of the stable.

A groom took control of the horse. Jamie slid down from his back and fished out a carrot from his pocket to feed to him. Phaeton chewed it, nodding his head and dropping bits of carrot onto the ground. Jamie laughed and patted his shoulder gently before heading off toward the manor.

The sun had settled down onto the horizon by the time he entered the house. He passed by a cluster of servants just inside and then went through the halls, up the stairs until he came to the main hall.

The Marquess of Marrenfort stood beside the main staircase. He was of middling height, indiscriminately colored hair going gray, gray eyes…an easily overlooked man. Yet Jamie knew better than to underestimate his father.

"Ah. Jamie. You're back."

"Yes, Father."

"Where's Edwin?"

"I don't know; he raced on ahead."

"Edwin! Hey there." He stopped a servant, "Find Lord Ashton and tell him to come here."

The girl started and nodded, then scuttled off up the stairs toward Edwin's room.

Jamie frowned a little. "What is it?"

Just then Edwin pounded down the stairs, brow creased and expression set. "Yes, here I am."

"Ah! Lady Montington and her daughter are

coming in a few days. You remember Cassandra—she is a great hunter, and I thought we would mount a hunt while she is here. She is riding her horse over to stable with ours."

"I will be leaving for Southampton tomorrow," Jamie said.

"Yes, yes, you won't be here, not that you would have ridden to the hounds if you were." The marquess's voice held a note of disapproval and Jamie's face went warm at the slight.

"Well, then I shall go make sure my trunk is completely packed."

His father waved him off and turned to Edwin. Jamie climbed the stairs and found his valet in the process of packing his trunk. He looked at the uniforms and a surge of pride filled him at serving his country in such a manner. A cold touch of fear tingled down his spine at the thought of getting on another ship, however, and sweat broke out on his brow. He had been aboard ships ever since, but there was something about being on a warship laden with cannon and powder just ready to blow.

He shook himself and wiped a hand across his forehead. He would have to conquer this—the navy would not give him any more time to recover. It was now or never...

It would be now.

He toyed with the thought of writing to Anne, but what would he say? There was nothing she didn't already know, and his father would frown on such a correspondence. Of course, his father would frown on most anything he did...

He glanced at the gilt clock on the dark wood

mantle and realized he needed to dress for supper. His valet selected a clean shirt and dark blue waistcoat, and Jamie stripped out of his afternoon clothes. He pulled on clean breeches and buttoned up the waistcoat before slipping on his shoes and jacket. He sat back and looked around at his room, wondering how long he'd be gone this time.

Dressed and brushed in time for the supper gong, he made his way down the stairs to the dining room. His father insisted on using the expansive space though it was only the three of them. He walked down the length of the table to his spot and stood waiting for his brother and father. They both came in together after a few minutes, his brother still frowning into his drink. Jamie wondered if father had been hammering him about duty and marriage again.

They progressed silently through the courses. Edwin drank more than his fair share of wine. Jamie tried to catch his eye, but failed as his brother seemed intent upon his glass.

Their father had noticed Edwin's libations and carefully set his fork down. "Edwin, I think you've had enough "

"I disagree." Then he motioned for it to be refilled.

The marquess slashed his hand to stop the servant and Edwin turned an ugly stare on him. "I am of age, Father. Well over it, I might add."

"You have yet to act your age."

Edwin dropped his napkin on the table and stormed off.

The marquess closed his eyes. "Go check on your brother. I shouldn't have to tell you."

"Yes, sir."

Jamie rose and went after Edwin, checking with servants to trace his path. Finally, he found himself out in the rose garden. His brother stood in the moonlight, just by the fountain.

Jamie stood in silence beside his brother for a few minutes. Finally, Edwin blew out a harsh breath.

"You're damned lucky, Jamie. No one is harping on you to be something you aren't. You can just be Jamie, second son, lieutenant of whatever."

"Whereas you are the Earl of Ashton, heir apparent of the Marquess of Marrenfort."

"What the hell good are these titles anyway? It seems terribly outdated and even unfair. Why the eldest son? Why me?"

Jamie sighed. "You won by order of your birth. It does seem unfair, but someone has to inherit."

Edwin blew out another breath. "I'd much rather it had been you."

"Wishing won't change the way things are."

Hands on hips, he regarded the fountain and his shoulders dropped. "Sorry, brother. I don't know why I get in these moods. Shouldn't have poked Father and all that. I just... I don't know."

Jamie placed a hand on his shoulder. "It's all right. You have a lot of pressure on you."

"As do you, going off to war. Be careful this time." He looked at Jamie with a slight frown.

"I will. You too—no jumping Gypsy's Gate."

Edwin laughed shortly. "You sound like Mother!"

"I'll take that as a good thing."

They headed back toward the house, rambling along companionably.

"How long will it take you to get to Portsmouth?"

"Southampton. Two days. Not too bad."

Edwin was silent for a moment. "I know I tease you a lot, but deep down I respect you, Jamie. You're a good man."

Jamie's eyebrows arched, and he glanced over at his brother who stared at the moon. "Thank you, Edwin. I feel the same about you."

Edwin snorted. "You're just saying that now. I'm not a bad man…but I am not like you."

Jamie could not argue with that, and they went up the stairs together to the house. From the woods came the lonely cry of a fox. It echoed from the direction of Gypsy's Gate, then faded into the night.

Jamie paused for a moment before going in, then followed his brother.

Chapter Five

Anne twitched her skirt out of the way and blew out an exasperated breath. She disliked riding sidesaddle and wearing a riding habit. It felt confining and restrictive when she wanted to be able to feel the horse's response directly. Still, she rode sedately toward Marrenfort where the rest of the riders were assembling.

She nodded toward Cassandra and pulled up next to her. The rest of the company milled about, calming nervous mounts or talking quietly amongst themselves. Cassandra smiled at her, dressed in her deep black riding habit which set off her dark eyes and hair. Anne knew her own dark blue skirt and jacket looked stunning against the gray-flecked white of her horse. The hounds ran to and fro, sniffing and the Master of the Hounds blew his horn to signal the start of the hunt.

It had been two weeks since Jamie had returned to his ship in Southampton. Anne wondered where he was. Had they sailed yet? She wished she had gotten an idea of his itinerary while he'd been home. But then, perhaps he didn't know.

Sighing, she tried to focus on the hunt at hand. Everyone was watching the dogs as they moved out, trying to catch the scent. Suddenly, baying broke through the stillness of the morning and the dogs raced off.

Edwin surged to the front instantly and Cassandra waved at Anne as she urged her horse into a canter behind the hounds. Anne followed at a slow pace. She had sided with Jamie when he objected to the hunt, but out of respect for the marquess had decided to ride far to the back. Now she reined her horse back to a trot, keeping the company in view. There was another outbreak of baying, and she knew the hounds had caught a fresher scent.

She moved into a canter now, cutting across a field to keep them in view. The dogs dashed toward a copse of trees on the hill, with the horses and riders in hot pursuit. She jumped a low hedge and galloped across the field, as the line of riders disappeared into the woods beside the stream. She pulled her horse to a halt and waited until the company came back into view.

Time seemed to stand still. The air did not move across her; only a bird's song interrupted her quiet. She did not know how long she waited, looking down the rise over the patchwork countryside, but a disturbance broke out by the eastern end of the woods and the horn blasted again as the fox doubled back.

The fox burst out of the woods, with the hounds following. The red coated Master was just behind with the leaders of the company. She frowned, looking for Edwin, only to find him farther back in the grouping. He broke free, and cut across toward Gypsy's Gate.

The wet ground beside the little stream gave way as his mount jumped and the horse fell short of the posts. It went down in a tangle of legs and briars, with Edwin lost in their midst, framed by the trees.

Anne spurred her horse toward him and was off in an instant once they had reached the edge of the gate.

She rushed forward through the brush, briars pulling at her skirt until she found the unmoving form of her friend. Kneeling beside him, she reached out as others now joined her. His neck was twisted impossibly to the side, and he lay terribly still. Voices broke out around her, but she couldn't understand what anyone was saying.

She only knew that Edwin was dead.

Suddenly she was pushed aside as the Marquess of Marrenfort rushed forward. He stood staring down at the crumpled form of his son. Anne reached tentatively forward for his arm. He resisted for a moment, then let her pull him backward from the scene. The marquess stared off with his colorless eyes and then looked at her.

"I'm so sorry Anne."

"Oh no, sir. It is I who am sorry. Your son was a good man."

The marquess's voice caught, and he simply nodded.

The afternoon sped by in a haze of waiting, then rapid activity, then more waiting. Edwin's body was collected and carried toward the house. He was taken to his room and laid out. The doctor confirmed what everyone knew, the heir to Marrenfort was gone.

As the activity hummed about Marrenfort, Anne slipped out and found her horse, then headed off across the fields to the track along the stream. She followed it until she came to the drive of Enniston, before heading toward the road. Her horse was determined to go towards the stables, but Anne urged her down the drive. It was nearly half an hour later that she pulled up before the little cottage behind the fields.

She slipped down from her horse, just as the door

opened and Bessie came out. She smiled at her, looking around and frowning when she did not see Edwin.

"Lady Anne, welcome." There was a question in her voice.

"Bessie, something terrible has happened…"

Bessie stilled, then suddenly shouted, "Mamma! Mamma, come here!"

After a moment, Mrs. Oldham bustled out of the cottage, "What you on about, Bess?"

But Bessie simply reached over, grasped her mother's hand, and swallowed. "Now, miss. Now."

Tears sprang into her eyes, the first since Edwin had died. "Edwin had an accident. He has died. I'm so sorry…"

Bessie wailed and crumpled as her mother caught her. Anne simply shook her head.

"I'm so sorry. I'm so sorry."

Slowly, she climbed back onto her horse's back and rode in a daze back toward her home. The woods rang with the sounds of birds and insects, and yet she heard only Bessie's howl of pain and loss. What she would feel if Jamie were killed in battle somewhere?

Her chest clenched and she choked from the sudden pressure and pain the very thought brought. *Surely they will bring him home now!*

The horse ambled to the Enniston stables. She slid gratefully down and headed for her room so she could shed the riding habit. She went through her wardrobe to find a suitable dress and finally chose her smoky gray afternoon dress. It would have to do for consoling the Marrenforts. As she came downstairs, she met her father just coming in. She pulled up short and stared at him. How to tell him the news?

"Father," she said loudly.

"Eh? What?"

"We must go to Marrenfort."

He glanced at the clock and squinted. "Nonsense."

"Edwin is dead."

Her father stared. "What did Edwin say? Has he done something to you? I'll—"

"He's dead!" she cried, tears finally springing from her eyes. "He's dead, I watched him fall…" She started to fall to her knees when her father caught her up.

"There, now, there. Get hold of yourself now." He patted her awkwardly as he supported her.

She sniffed and blew her nose in her handkerchief. Drying her eyes, only to wet them once more, she dragged in a ragged breath. Finally, her father held out his large handkerchief and she clutched it to her face, dabbing the tears as they fell.

"You're right; we must call on the Hannigans. Come."

He hailed a servant to have their carriage readied and took her to the parlor where they could watch for it. In due time the carriage arrived. It was a long, silent drive to Marrenfort.

Anne noted that all the hunters and hounds were now gone. They trudged up to the front step and rang the bell. The butler greeted and announced them and stood back. The Marquess of Marrenfort advanced, the black he wore making him seem to fade even more into the background. He greeted them, then took Anne's hands,

"I know how much you meant to him, my dear. Thank you for making him so happy."

They think we were a couple!

"Thank you, Lord Marrenfort. I feel his loss greatly."

"Come, my dear. I'll take you to him."

Panic rose as he took her arm and led her up the stairs. They turned to the left to follow the hall down to a door that opened. An older man dressed in black bowed to Lord Marrenfort and stood aside as Anne stepped into the room.

The drapes were drawn, and the only light came from the candles burning throughout the room. Edwin lay there, clean, and his neck straightened. His head was cradled on the pillow and his eyes were closed as though in sleep. His skin had taken on a waxy hue, and one side of his face still held the scratches from the brush he had fallen upon.

"Oh…" She sighed and turned abruptly away.

Lord Marrenfort patted her back and led her back out of the room.

"There, my dear. It's all right."

They returned to the main floor and crossed to the large parlor. A tea cart stood to one side. The servants had readied the room for mourners. Her father sat with a cup of tea and a small cucumber sandwich in one hand. He stood as they entered the room, and set the sandwich on a small plate and the cup on its saucer.

"Well, Anne?" he thundered.

"I am well, Father."

"Good, good. And you, Marrenfort?"

"Busy, you know. Things to arrange."

"Jamie must be brought home," Anne said.

The marquess' eyebrows shot up, then he frowned a little. "James? Yes, yes I suppose so. God knows where he is, though."

"The navy will know…if you write to them."

The marquess patted her shoulder, "Never you fear, my dear. All will be well."

All Anne could think of was that soon Jamie would be home, and that perhaps he would have to stay, safe, far from the war. Tears of relief pressed forward, and she pulled out her handkerchief to wipe them away. She went to the cart and poured herself some tea to give her an excuse to turn her back on the two peers.

She stared down at the cup in her hand and noted it shook. Gulping in a breath, she fought to steady her nerves and lowered herself upon the velvet settee. She stared around the familiar room through reddened eyes, with only one thought.

Jamie was coming home.

Her father was talking some platitude that she doubted would be welcome. With a final sip, she finished her tea and rose as it still rattled in its saucer on the table.

"Come, Father. We must leave Lord Marrenfort to his plans. Sir, please call on us if there is anything we can do."

"Of course, of course. Anything…" her father said.

Lord Marrenfort thanked them and followed them to the door. When Anne looked back from her seat in the carriage, he still stood alone on the front step.

She was silent as they rode back. Her father made one or two observations that she barely heard. All she could think of was the funeral to be got through—with everyone thinking she was mourning a betrothed, when in truth she had lost a friend.

A friend who had tied her to a secret.

What was she to do about that? She wished Jamie was there so she could ask him about it. Surely he would know what was best.

He always seemed to know best.

Chapter Six

The sun stood high in the blue expanse, light filtering through a few white clouds scattered about. Seagulls flew overhead, a sign they were near port and out of danger. The French would not sail this close to Portugal.

Men pulled on ropes beside him, raising the topsails to slow the ship. A few scampered lithely up to secure the sails and Jamie shielded his eyes to watch them. A fishing vessel sailed past, her deck loaded with baskets of fish bound for the market. The fishermen mock-saluted them then broke into laughter, waving cheerfully.

The air filled with sound as they neared port. Soon they edged closer as more sails were raised and tied down and the ship coasted gently into her berth, lines cast and caught and secured. They had arrived, and would be in port for some days.

The first day back on ship had been difficult. He'd sweated every time he'd been near the point on the ship where the *Dorchester* had blown apart. He'd found himself avoiding that section unless absolutely necessary, as it was now.

Jamie swallowed against the tightness in his chest and exhaled slowly to calm his nerves. He was looking forward to being on land again. The past couple of weeks had made him question his career plans somewhat.

And yet, he thrived in this environment. The work, the camaraderie, the discipline—all played to his strengths and pushed him to better himself. His pride grew, pride in himself and his abilities. He had grown into his own man as a naval officer, and he was proud of that.

He grabbed a line and pulled with the rest of the crew to draw the ship into her place. It wasn't until all were tied securely that the gangplank was lowered.

The captain called his officers close and said a few terse words. The sailors worked to finish fitting up the ship and Jamie found himself at a loose end. He stepped gratefully down the gangplank into a new world.

All around him people bustled. Carts full of fish lined the dock. Women in scarves and colorful skirts meandered along, poking the fish and haggling with the mongers. Sound filled the air, pulsing in words he did not understand. The smell of the sea, fish, and an oily undercurrent accosted him as he moved along. He looked down and a pair of children stared at him from behind a blue-checked skirt. He smiled and lifted a hand. Their eyes widened as they ducked back behind the wall of cloth.

He chuckled and gazed around, heading aimlessly toward the street leading from the wharf. Shops and vendors with barrows filled with goods lined the street. Donkeys pulling low carts mingled with men on horseback and people milling about. Jamie could not help smiling.

The sun shone bright, and the air moved around him gently, only slightly tinged with cold. It felt glorious after weeks on the frigid sea. He felt strangely free, despite the constant tug of Anne's memory.

Suddenly he caught sight of her, and his heart jumped in his chest as the sunlight reflected white-gold off the top of her head. When he looked more closely, however, he saw it was another woman, dressed in pink and blue, with blonde hair and dark eyes, struggling with a dark-haired man and yelling.

"*Ajuda!*"

Jamie ran, pushing through the throng gathered around the fighting couple. He erupted through the ring and pushed the man back away from the woman. She stood with her back to the crowd as the man surged forward to swing a fist at Jamie, who ducked backward and replied with his own fist to the man's jaw. He dropped like a stone and lay senseless on the brick pavement.

The woman screamed and knelt to lay her ear against the man's chest. She must have heard a heartbeat for she leaned back and spoke to the men standing around. They began to drag him to a bench where he was laid out and left. She began to pick up scattered goods that had fallen from her basket.

Jamie bent to help, picking up a fish that had come partly free of its wrapping and a loaf of bread. He laid them into her basket and looked at her for the first time. She was clearly older than him, and a young boy came up and clung to her. She lifted him in her arms and Jamie hefted the basket for her.

She smiled and said, "Inglis?" He nodded and she said, "*Obrigado*. My *Inglis* small."

He tapped himself on the chest. "Lieutenant Hannigan."

"Ah! Beatriz Alvarenga." She pointed to the man

on the bench and said, "João Alvarenga." She patted the little boy and gave him a cuddle saying, "Francisco."

He smiled out one side of his mouth and said, "Hello."

Motioning her on and lifting the basket, he trailed after her as she wove through the crowd and meandered through the streets to a small house with a pig in the yard. He followed her inside and set the basket down on a table. She gestured for him to sit and he did so. She picked up a bowl and went to a large pot hanging above the fire. She ladled out a stew into the bowl and handed it to him with a wooden spoon.

"*Cozido*," she said, before dipping some for herself and the boy.

They all ate in silence, Jamie pleasantly surprised by the mixture of flavors that cascaded through his mouth. He drank the weak beer she had set before him and felt satisfied by the hearty meal. Rising, he thanked her and headed for the door, only to see the ragged figure of João Alvarenga coming along the street.

Beatriz came to the door and stood with her hands on her hips as he approached. He ignored Jamie, kissed her on the cheek and moved past them to a bed behind a curtain, where he collapsed with a sigh. Jamie had the feeling that the day's events had repeated often over the years.

Beatriz rolled her eyes and waved Jamie off with a smile. He hesitated leaving her alone with João, but she waved him on again and he left. Casting around for his bearings, he set off toward the tall masts showing over the buildings in the distance.

By the time he reached the docks the day had waned, and the shadows were long. The carts and barrows were mostly gone, and only a few remained. He made his way toward the *H.M.S. Waynflete*, pausing on the gangplank as the old fear gripped him. His gaze went to the area under the middle of the deck where the powder was stored, and his heart missed a beat as his chest tightened. As he stepped onto the deck, he set his foot down gingerly as though he were stepping on a bomb.

"Hannigan!"

Jamie jumped and spun to find the captain approaching. St. John Ellis's tall, spare figure came close and stopped.

"Where were you, lieutenant?"

"I went for a walk, got involved in a domestic dispute."

"I heard an officer was in a fight, was that you?"

"Yes, sir."

"Can't have that. Learn to stay out of local business."

"It was a woman being attacked by a man, sir."

"Probably a husband and wife arguing. Nothing to concern you."

Not wanting to acknowledge this was the truth, Jamie simply said, "Yes, sir."

"Confined to quarters for the rest of our stay here."

"Yes, sir." Jamie nodded and made his way to his cabin.

Built beneath the captain's rooms, it was a narrow room with just enough space for a bunk and a trunk. There was a large shelf over the bunk which held a few books and a shaving mirror, but little else. He sighed and looked out the window, watching the ship next to them for a moment before staring at the wooden wall that separated his cabin from the next.

Confined to quarters for days. Jamie leaned back on his narrow bed. He closed his eyes and wondered what Anne was doing—if she and Edwin had taken another ride in his brother's barouche without a chaperone.

His fist clenched at the thought, and he realized he had bruised his hand in the fight with João. Rubbing it lightly with his other hand, the pain faded in comparison to what he felt at the thought of Anne with someone else.

He swung his legs off the bunk and sat there, head in hands, trying to master the feelings pounding in his chest and spinning through his head. How long had he loved her? A long time, now that he thought about it. This feeling went back years. Was this why no other woman had ever been good enough?

Looking up at the wall again he envisioned Anne, and swallowed against the emotion that caught him. But Anne was back in England, at Enniston, right next door to Marrenfort where Edwin was...

He stood roughly, then paced the length of his cabin, coming up short in front of the window. He leaned against it, willing it to disappear and set him free. He would be days in here, shut away with only infrequent visits to the head. Closing his eyes he turned away and reached up to pull a book down. Without looking at it he sat back down and thumped it on his knee mindlessly. Finally, with a sigh, he opened it up and began to read, though his attention slipped with each sound from outside his little cabin.

Steps sounded outside and a knock rattled the door. IIc opened it, to see a young midshipman there with a letter in his hand.

"This just came in on the *Wiltshire*."

Jamie took the letter and opened it. The missive was short, but one sentence stood out in it:

Regret to inform you of your brother's death...

His breath caught in his chest. Edwin, gone? But what did that mean? How? He continued reading about a hunt and a jump... Had he jumped Gypsy's Gate? Why? What was he to do? He noted the next sentence which stated that his father wanted him home, immediately. He looked up but the midshipman was gone. He leaned out, listening for someone to come near him and finally stepped out, looking for the captain.

He found him in his rooms, working with a map. Captain Ellis frowned to see Jamie but before he could bark out a response, Jamie held out the open letter.

"I've just received this from the Naval Commission. My father has requested that I return home."

"What the devil for?"

"I...I am the last living heir."

The captain went still. He looked down for a moment and then up. "I'm sorry, Hannigan. Never easy getting bad news at sea."

"No, sir."

"I take it you are resigning your commission as of today?"

"I...no. Must I?"

There was a ghost of a smile on Captain Ellis's face. "Not yet, anyway. Well, you can consider yourself confined to the ship instead of quarters until we find you a vessel to travel back on."

"Yes, sir. Thank you."

Jamie headed out onto the deck. He stood at the rail, looking out over the harbor toward the northwest where England, and home, lay. He wondered when he would be sent home, and what he would do in the meantime.

****

Two days later came the arrival of the *H.M.S. Belmont* into harbor. Headed north to Southampton, it was quickly decided that Jamie would join the crew to travel home. The captain, a short, apoplectic man, looked Jamie up and down without a word.

"Are you an officer or not?"

"Sir?"

"Are you resigning or staying in?"

"I…I don't know, sir. Staying I hope."

"What will your papa say about that?" he sneered.

"I don't know."

"Well, see that you stay out of the way of the real officers who serve England."

"Er…yes of course. Sir."

Admiral Moster turned from Jamie, ordering a midshipman to show him to his quarters. Jamie followed the fellow who led him to an empty officer's bunk. He sat down on the edge of the bed and stared at the wall, for there was no porthole or window. He was in a dashed difficult place. He had initially thought he must resign his commission, but now wondered if that was actually necessary. Why couldn't he stay in the navy? What did it matter that he was the last living heir?

His chest constricted. Edwin… Edwin was gone, and he must go home to see to his father's needs. And then, there was Anne…

How was she taking the loss of Edwin? What must she be enduring? Had she been there when he had taken his last fall?

Anger shot through him suddenly, anger at his brother for being so foolhardy as to jump Gypsy's Gate knowing the dangers. Now he was gone, and they were left to suffer as a result. He struggled to quell his feelings, sensitive to the fact that his brother had paid a dear price for his foolhardiness.

But what now? How would his father handle this—his favorite child gone? Jamie closed his eyes and shook his head slowly for this would break the marquess. Then he considered what it meant for him, and he frowned. He must now take on the Ashton title and the role of eldest son. How was he to do that?

He was simply a lieutenant…

Chapter Seven

Anne rounded the edge of the woods and spurred her horse to a gallop. Moving in time with her horse's body she squinted against the cold wind. Her eyes watered. Before her horse started to blow hard, she pulled her up and slowed to a walk.

The village of Brumley lay at the bottom of the vale. She paused for a moment to stare down at it before heading off once more toward the southern end of town. There, a small farm stood behind stonewalled pastures. She rode down toward the main road and approached the house from the front to keep from scattering sheep and the sleepy cows. A pair of pigs grunted in their pen and Anne looked up to see her mother wielding a hoe in the garden.

The scene hurt her, for some reason. Not that the work was beneath her, but simply that her mother had always been so delicate, almost ethereal. It didn't fit her somehow.

It took a moment for Evelyn Kingsley to see her, and when she did, she raised her hand and waved, quickly setting down the hoe. She lifted the dark skirt then headed toward her, adjusting her shawl.

"My girl! What a surprise!" Evelyn dusted her hands. "My dear, what are you wearing?"

Anne looked down at her skirt and bit her lip. "My older riding habit. I'm not out to impress anyone."

"Yes, my dear. But still. That jacket is a bit tattered." She adjusted her patched short coat and twitched her skirt.

Anne wanted desperately to scream at her. *Why?* She stood still while her mother kissed her and then stood back to cast her gaze over her.

"Well I think you are even taller."

"Oh, Mother, I don't think so. At least all my clothes still fit me as usual. What were you doing in the garden?"

"Digging some potatoes for supper. John likes them, and we have a bit of steak tonight as the old bull was butchered last week."

"I see. It sounds disagreeable."

"Yes dear, but then I didn't have much to do with it."

Anne smiled. "I was talking about the potatoes."

Evelyn's eyes crinkled as she smiled.

"How is your cooking?"

"Well, Mrs. Magruddy comes once a week to help me plan and to do the meals. But, oh! It is wonderful to see you!"

Anne knew that her mother had almost no company in the little village. All of society, low and high, had forsaken her. All but the indomitable Mrs. Magruddy who had taken pity on John Havers's woman.

Unable to marry while her husband still lived, Evelyn Kingsley had simply reverted to her maiden name and lived as John Havers' common-law wife. Anne noted new lines about the face of her mother, born of hard work and trials, and she tightened her grip on her mother's arm.

They went into the stone cottage with its large wooden beams and low ceilings. A bright fire burned in the fireplace, with a pot hanging close to the flames. Evelyn used a corner of her apron to lift the lid and check the contents. Then she went to the kitchen and returned with a kettle to hang over the fire as well.

"Kettle is still warm, so it won't be long. Sit, Anne!"

Anne sat on the worn chair near the fire. Her mother sat in the other chair. Once upon a time servants and cooks attended her, but here she was, weighed down with work and cut off from all society…all for love?

Evelyn sighed and then her chin lifted a little as though she could read Anne's mind. "I am truly happy, Anne. I have no regrets. Well…I have one. I miss you."

"I miss you, too. Is there anything you need?"

Evelyn chuckled. "Another hand or two? I never knew how much work the servants put in for our comfort."

"Yes, that is true. Don't you miss that?"

Evelyn was silent for a moment. "Yes and no. I used to be so bored. There is only so much needlework and visiting one can do. My mind would wander, and I was quite lonely much of the time."

"Aren't you lonely now?"

"Well, now I have John. I know you can't understand, my dear. But he makes me feel alive and valued…and that makes it worth the while."

Anne sat staring into the fire, thinking. She wondered what she would be willing to do for Jamie. Would she leave her home and friends to follow him anywhere? In her heart she knew the answer. "I think I may understand, a little."

"Now, my dear, are you quite recovered from Lord Ashton's death?"

Anne's head snapped up and she took the cup her mother pressed upon her. "Oh, I... yes. The funeral was rather awful..."

Her mother frowned a little and quirked her head. "I had always wondered... I mean, you two were rather thrown together..."

"I wasn't in love with Edwin." Anne said bluntly.

Her mother let loose a sigh. "I am glad to hear that. I had worried about the effect upon you."

"No... not Edwin."

"Jamie?"

Anne's gaze lifted to her mother and her mouth parted, but no sound came out.

"It's all right, Anne. I always liked Jamie. More stable, and dependable. Quiet strength. He is a good man."

Anne sipped her tea and stared down as the leaves swirled. "We are expecting him home soon."

"I imagine the navy had a hard time getting a message to him."

"Yes. I hope they found him."

Evelyn gave a little laugh. "Well, dear. I'm sure our navy knew right where to put their hand upon him."

Anne smiled. "It's just, I worry so. The French and all..."

"I understand. He puts himself in danger, and after that close shave..."

"Yes, exactly. And he isn't right, yet. It still haunts him. And yet he goes back, ready to fight."

"As I said, a good man."

Anne set her cup down and stood. "It is late and I didn't tell anyone I was coming here. I should get back."

Evelyn rose and hugged her. "Thank you for coming, you have made this day to shine for me."

"Oh, Mother…" Anne fought a tear from falling.

"None of that. I am happy, and you are always welcome."

Anne sniffed and nodded, impulsively hugging her mother again before turning to go. Evelyn followed her until she had climbed onto her horse. They shared a long look before Anne reined her horse around and headed off.

She fought the urge to look back, and steered her horse around the outbuildings and up the side of the hill. Once she reached the top, she looked back to see her mother standing where she had left her. She lifted a hand and Evelyn did the same, before she went back into the house.

Anne urged her horse into a canter, and they rocked gently over the fields up to the edge of the woods. The day had remained cloudy and cold, the kind of cold that clings to every exposed part. She was grateful for her gloves and only wished she had thought to bring a scarf for her neck.

They made it back to the stables and she slid down gratefully to walk back to the manor. The house was quiet, just a maid adding more coal to the fire in the parlor as Anne passed by on her way to her room. Once there, she unbuttoned her jacket and undressed, then pulled a periwinkle afternoon dress out. Her maid arrived and helped her fasten her gown before picking up the riding habit and taking it off to clean.

Anne wandered down to the parlor and went to the harp standing in the corner. She brushed a hand across the strings and then plucked out a simple tune before switching to another, more complex one. She stopped, and the strings continued to hum as the melody died away in the room.

Leaning her head down against the neck of the harp she wondered where Jamie was and when he would be home. Her heart ached with fear that the message had reached him too late and that he, too, was gone.

A cry stopped in her throat, nearly choking her and she stood, roughly. She rushed out from the room and into the main hall only to see her father coming toward her with a letter in his hand.

"Anne! Ah, there you are."

"What is it?"

"My sister Constance is coming with her daughter Adeline. They'll be here for a fortnight starting Sunday. What rooms shall we put them in?"

"Well, Constance likes the Rose Room. We'll put Addie in the Green."

"Good, good. I can leave you to it, then? Speak to the housekeeper, the cook, and all that?"

"Yes, Father. I will handle it all."

"Good, good!"

He headed back toward his room, and she glanced around for some sign of the housekeeper. She trotted downstairs to find her in her corner conferring with the cook.

"Mrs. Stevens, my aunt and her daughter will be coming this Sunday for a fortnight. I imagine they will have their maids with them and their driver and groom. I was thinking we would put my aunt into the Rose

Room and her daughter in the Green. I am assuming you will find lodging for their servants."

"Oh, of course. We'll take care of it. I may have to double up the maids a bit to fit them all."

"I'll trust your judgement. Mrs. Jones, is there anything you need as far as meals?"

"No, miss. I don't recall anything special with either of them."

"Lady Oglefort likes squab."

"Ah yes! We can manage that."

Anne nodded to them both and made her way back up the stairs. The hustle and movement of bodies stopped as she entered the main area, and it went quiet. Her father would be in his room. It was Tuesday, which meant his steward would be there with him going over accounts. She decided to avoid that section of the house.

She went to the garden and wandered along the different rose bushes. There would be no more flowers until spring, but she meandered along, remembering times spent with her mother in that very way. The garden itself was a brainchild of Evelyn, and Anne missed her most when she was out in it.

Her mind went back the two years when her mother had declared her intention of leaving. She had stood, back ramrod straight, and made the declaration before she and her father. Anne remembered freezing, wondering how she had missed the hints, but then it was shortly after she had been presented, and her mind had been full of that.

She realized she had stopped and stood next to one of the oldest rose bushes in the garden, one planted by her grandfather. Her mother had never asked her to go with her, and yet she knew that her presence would have made her mother's happiness complete. Still, she had no connection to John, only resentment that he had taken her mother away. *Perhaps I just disliked my own life being upset and took that out on him.*

What did she know about John? His mother was the daughter of a gentlewoman, and he had grown up on the estate, farming with his father. He and her mother would have met any number of times once she came to live there. When had their affair started? How had they met? She had never asked her mother. Maybe she hadn't been ready to find out.

****

Sunday came, and with it her aunt and cousin. The Honorable Adeline Oglefort was a tall, dark-haired beauty who always looked exquisitely dressed. Anne felt quite shabby in her white linen frock.

Addie embraced her and held her back. "Oh my dear! I haven't seen that style in over a year, yet you wear it beautifully!"

Anne tried to smile. "Your dress is just lovely."

"Oh, well I wanted something comfortable to travel in, you know. Tell me, are we going to see the newest Lord Ashton?"

Anne's eyes flew wide, "You mean Jamie? He is on his way back from the sea, but we don't know when he will arrive."

Addie's expression froze, but she recovered. "Well, we are nice and snug here aren't we! And a whole fortnight to scheme and talk. I am so sorry about your beau. What a dreadful loss."

"Oh, Edwin was not my beau."

"Well, I know no one ever said so, but everyone

knew."

"But, he wasn't."

"Then who?"

"I have no beau."

Addie's eyebrows met. But then her face cleared "Ha! We shall see. Come, my dear, show me to my room so I can get cleaned up and into something decent."

Anne led her up the stairs and into the Green Room. The wood wainscot and furniture were tempered with flowered curtains with broad green leaves and a green counterpane. Addie looked around and turned to Anne, flashing her eyes.

"Lovely. Now leave me. But where is my maid?"

"I'll send a message for her to join you."

"Yes, do! Ta."

Anne found herself pushed gently from the room and the door closed behind her. Eyes wide in disbelief, she went to the end of the hall and into her room. Light shone in from the windows, and a fire burned in the grate, warming the room against the coming winter. She caught a glimpse of herself in the mirror and turned this way and that to evaluate her dress. The waist was perhaps a tad higher than was currently fashionable, and the sleeves a little plain, but all-in-all it was one of her favorite dresses. She picked up a sash and tied it around the high waist, masking it slightly. She changed her necklace to a plain topaz drop and matching earrings. That and the blue sash added just enough color to bring out her eyes. Whether or not she was fashionable, she thought she looked well.

Going downstairs to the drawing room, she heard the bell ring and paused for a moment on the stairs.

Lifting her skirt, she trotted deftly down and rounded the corner to see who had come.

And came face to face with Jamie!

Chapter Eight

Jamie had traveled for weeks to reach home. First had come the long ride home on the *H.M.S. Belmont*. Its captain had taken an instant dislike to Jamie and treated him as less than a midshipman. When they had finally arrived in Southampton, he had been relieved to transfer to the mail.

The trip by mail was long, uncomfortable, and tedious, but finally he had arrived in Brumley and hired a horse to carry him home. While a groom returned the horse, he had found his father in the little chapel.

"Father?"

The marquess spun slowly, his face expressionless. "It's you, is it?"

"Yes, I'm home."

His father simply turned away. James slowly approached and stood beside him at the low altar.

"Father, I'm so sorry."

Gruffly, the marquess said, "Yes, yes. But now you're the heir. You need to start acting like it."

"I shall try, sir."

The marquess's head dropped and his eyes closed. "I wish to God you had been on that horse instead."

Something cold encircled Jamie's heart. "If I had, I wouldn't have been jumping Gypsy's Gate."

The marquess's head snapped up and he glared at Jamie. "Get out."

"Yes, sir."

His father's voice followed him, "You're to leave the navy."

"I shall certainly consider it, sir."

He stalked out and blew out a breath. His father's antipathy had never been more than veiled, but now seemed ready to erupt. That his favorite child had died while Jamie still lived seemed to be almost more than the marquess could accept.

Jamie looked down at his somewhat rumpled clothes and sighed. He headed toward the stables and ordered his horse saddled and readied. Then he jumped astride Phaeton and sped away from Marrenfort.

Enniston rose over the hill, and he urged Phaeton into a quick canter. When he reached the front door, he hopped down and took the steps three at a time before pulling the cord to ring the bell. It opened. He caught movement out of the corner of his eye and went instinctively toward it.

And had found Anne.

They stared at one another, then with a cry she started forward as though to embrace him before restraining herself. Without thinking he reached out, pulled her to him, and pressed his lips down on her open mouth.

She sighed and her eyes closed as he kissed her. After a moment they pulled apart, each breathless. Jamie's gaze roved over her face, and he brushed a strand of her hair aside.

"Anne," he whispered.

"Oh, Jamie. You're safe."

"Yes. For now."

She frowned and pushed back from him, "You

aren't going back, are you?"

"I don't know. I haven't resigned my commission yet."

"But you are needed here."

Jamie sighed and pulled away. "I doubt that. My father is perfectly capable of running the estate."

"But surely, as the heir—"

"Father isn't going to treat me like an heir. I'll be nothing but an unpleasant reminder of Edwin's loss."

"Surely not. He'll be so happy to have you."

"Anne, you know that isn't true."

"But, now that it's only you—"

"It will be worse. I think Father hates me now."

"No, that is harsh. It is difficult for him just now."

"Are you defending him? You know how he's treated me in the past."

"But that is the past. Now you are all he has."

He turned away and shook his head. "I thought you would understand."

"I'm trying to, but I am hoping for the best."

"You can hope, I know. If I stay it will be dashed difficult."

"Lord Ashton!" Elegantly attired in lilac silk, Addie floated in with her hand extended toward Jamie.

"Oh...I... Have we met?" He took her hand and bowed briefly over it.

Her face fell a little. She recovered though. "Last summer when I was visiting." She gently interposed herself between Anne and him, grasped his arm with her hands and pulled him into a walk with her. "Do let's take a turn. I have been longing to see the library. Surely you won't mind escorting me there."

He disengaged himself from her. "I must be going.

Goodbye, miss, er," He shifted his gaze to Anne and the tenor of his voice dropped. "Anne." His gaze lingered on her for a moment before all but running for the door.

Once free of the house, he vaulted onto Phaeton and urged him quickly to speed down the long, curving driveway.

"Idiot!" he said aloud as he rode.

He played the moment of their kiss over and over, only to berate himself. Their first kiss had led to their first near argument. Of course Anne, gentle-hearted as she was, would take his father's side. She had just watched him bury his eldest son, and had easily guessed at the grief barely hidden behind a wall of English fortitude. She had rarely seen him lash out at Jamie with cold, cutting remarks. That was always saved for when no one, save Edwin, was around.

Edwin. He allowed the horse to slow to a walk. Somehow it only seemed real now. The look on his father's face had confirmed it all. Edwin was dead. And now, he must carry the burden of the title and the future inheritance.

All the while bearing his father's antipathy.

He urged Phaeton to a trot. Marrenfort appeared as he came around the edge of the woods. The house looked peaceful, stolid and safe, the little pond before it still and mirror-like. A goose or duck scooted across it, leaving a line of ripples marring the surface. By the time he had dragged his concentration away, Phaeton had once again slowed to a walk.

He urged his horse to a trot and guided him toward the stables. A rumble sounded in the distance, and he noted the sky had darkened. His breath condensed into clouds that fell away with the wind. As another peal of thunder sounded, he spurred Phaeton to a canter.

A groom came up to take the bridle while Jamie slid out of the saddle. He stroked Phaeton's neck for a moment, delaying the time he would actually return to the manor. Finally, with a sigh, he headed off towards the hulking house that he called home.

The first strike of rain hit him before he made it indoors. By the time he burst into the downstairs entrance, his hair dripped rainwater. He shook his head and wiped his face before heading up the stairs to the main hall.

It was empty, and his boots rang on the old stone floor. To the right, down the distant hall, a light shone from his father's room. He went in the opposite direction down the long gallery. Rivulets of rain on the tall, mullioned windows cast shadows over the portraits arranged there. He strode along, seeking out his paternal grandfather from among the faces. It could have been his own that stared back at him. Tall, decisive, striking—everything his father was not. And when the current Lord Marrenfort looked at Jamie, he saw his father and felt once again all the old criticisms he'd endured.

Jamie blew out a breath in the dim light. Understanding the source of his father's antipathy did nothing to stop the pain. Deep longing welled up, longing for a father's love and for his brother to be returned. Two things he wanted more than anything…

Almost.

Anne's face appeared before him, and he knew that there he could find the happiness that had been so distant in his life. His heart quickened at the thought of a life with her at his side. But he'd made a mess of things.. How to fix it?

He did not know, but he knew he would try.

Miss Oglefort's presence had been an unhappy intrusion. He closed his eyes as he remembered her very pointed attentions. This would be awkward...

He glanced once more at his grandfather's portrait and headed back toward the main hall and the staircase leading to his room. It was a little early to dress for supper, but he went through the motions anyway, then sat down at the little desk and stared at the blotting paper for a moment. The light hit it in such a way that he could see the indentations of past writings there, ghostly impressions of previous thoughts and wishes. He bent his head and screwed up his eyes against the tears that threatened. Taking a breath, he pushed back and looked around.

It was a very ordinary room for the second son of a marquess. He rose and went to Edwin's room, looking at the distinctly royal aspect of it. Ancient tapestries covered the walls, though Marrenfort was only two hundred years old. A painting of the first Marquess of Marrenfort hung over the fireplace, which lay empty and cold. Edwin had always fancied a likeness to the "first gentleman" as he called him.

Jamie glanced over at the bed, knowing his dead brother had lain there. He went to it. One hand lay on the coverlet as he sighed. He missed him, and his throat tightened.

Blowing out a cleansing breath he turned, to find his father standing there.

"Come to gloat?"

"Never. How can you think that?"

"It looks as though you are surveying your

property."

"I don't want Edwin's room. I miss him!"

The marquess looked away. "What will you do?"

"About what?"

"The navy."

Jamie sighed. "I don't know."

"What isn't there to know? Resign your commission!"

"It isn't as simple as that."

"It is. You submit your letter and sell the commission. Come home to serve."

"Father, you can barely look at me. How would that actually work?"

"It is your duty as my son and heir."

"I have a duty to myself as well. I like the navy."

"Navy be damned!"

Jamie hadn't known what he would do until challenged on it. Now he turned to his father and stood his ground. "I am staying in and serving my country. I have a duty to her as well."

The marquess's mouth fell open and Jamie pushed past to go to his room. Once there, he opened the trunk which still held his uniforms. The front bell rang. The butler's footsteps clicked as he went to answer it and Jamie wondered if it was a note from Anne. He very nearly ran to see, but restrained himself and looked out the window at the dying rain.

After a few minutes, a knock sounded. A footman carrying a letter entered and handed it to him. He glanced down, recognizing Anne's handwriting and quickly opened it. Scanning the contents, he realized she was inviting him and his father to tea the following day. He refolded the letter and tapped it against his other hand. With a sigh, he went in search of his father.

He found him in his room, surrounded by his favorite things—a taxidermy mount of a pheasant in flight under glass, and several shelves of books and ledgers that went back to the beginning of Marrenfort. There were a large compass and sextant. The skin of a lion stretched out in front of the fireplace since his grandfather had brought it home from Africa. A painting of the manor hung over the fireplace, and a silhouette of his mother hung on the wall beside the door. Jamie noted that his father need only look up from his desk to see it.

"Yes?"

"We have been invited to tea at Enniston tomorrow. Lady Oglefort is there with her daughter."

The marquess grunted. "Very well. You may go, I will stay to go over some things with my steward."

"Yes, sir." Jamie left before his father could say anything else.

Supper was cold and silent. The marquess never acknowledged Jamie, and did not speak a word to anyone save a footman who served incorrectly. Jamie ate what was put in front of him, but could not have named it afterward. When they were done, they both left for their own rooms without wishing each other a good night.

Jamie closed his eyes at the thought of living like that for more than a few days.

****

Although the sun stayed behind a heavy blanket of clouds, it did not rain the following day and Jamie chose to ride over to Enniston on horseback. The road was muddy, and he steered Phaeton onto the grass wherever possible.

Anne was there to greet him, as well as Adelaide who simpered in a superior manner. Anne barely looked at him, and did not meet his eyes, something that grieved him deeply. He wanted to shout that he was sorry for whatever he had said or done. Anything to wipe away this terrible stiffness.

"My lord, please join us in the drawing room," said Anne.

Jamie almost looked to see if someone else was present, then realized Anne was calling him by his dead brother's title. He squirmed uncomfortably in his skin.

"Yes, of course."

He moved to follow. Adelaide grasped his elbow with her two hands and he was forced to slow down to match her step. As soon as they entered the room, he led her to a settee and left her while he went to a chair opposite. Anne sat down between them and served tea, still without really looking at him. Adelaide, however, kept up a running conversation.

"And you remember the Piedmonts? Their eldest girl is set to be married, but I don't think much of the groom. A baronet's son, and no estate. They say it is a love match, but I can't see the sense of it." She took a bite of cake and washed it down with a dainty sip of tea before continuing. "And then Brandt, the heir, went and got shot in a duel—as though anyone does those things anymore. They say he'll recover, but his left arm will never be right. And he was such a horseman!" She stared off, presumably remembering, before recalling herself. "And then there's me, little stay-at-home Addie all dressed up with never anywhere to go."

"I'm sure you have several engagements to

entertain you," Anne said.

"Well, yes, but there's me always pining for the comfort of home."

"Then, what is to stop you? I myself prefer to be at home, or with close friends, and avoid going out when I am not inclined," Jamie said, reaching for a biscuit.

"Ah, yes, but a gentleman is more in command of his actions. A woman must mold her behavior to the expectations of those around her."

"Surely not to such an extent," Jamie replied without really knowing what said. He was trying to peer past Anne's downward cast gaze.

Just then Lady Oglefort bustled in, her substantial size suiting her as she sat genteelly down beside her daughter.

"Ah! And what have you young things been discussing?"

"I was just catching them up on London gossip."

"Oh, my dear! Naughty girl! We shouldn't gossip, though some very marked things have happened. Did you tell them about Earl Danvers and the governess?"

"I hadn't gotten to that."

"Well! The earl had hired her for his nephew and niece—you know the ones he took in after their parents died in that ship that sunk coming home from Canada. There he was, all set to marry the Viscountess of Langley, when the governess comes up...well, you know, and the viscountess will no longer have him."

Anne set her cup down and rose. "Shall I play first? I know Addie is a superior musician, but I can make my offering." She went to the piano and sat down, seemed to struggle with the music for a moment before settling on one and arranging it to her liking.

Jamie listened to the music, his gaze never leaving her face. At one point, she looked up, into his eyes and her fingers faltered for a moment, then found their rhythm and continued on. She cast her gaze down, but not before a spark had ignited between them.

He almost smiled. He knew she had felt it as well. Whatever she had felt for Edwin might pass, and she could be his one day. The thought was intoxicating.

He suddenly realized her playing had stopped and belatedly began clapping. Addie sprang up and went to the piano as Anne left it. She slid into place and without glancing at the music available, began.

Her playing was very technical and correct, but lacked the feeling that had been present in Anne's playing. His spine crawled under the pressure of her exactness and pomposity of style. And yet, he struggled to maintain a placid face. He noted she glanced at him often, and he felt uncomfortable under her pointed regard.

She finally finished and this time he applauded immediately. She curtseyed and lingered as though hoping to be applied to continue playing. Anne said nothing and Jamie was just as silent. Finally, Addie rose and joined them, rubbing her fingers to attract attention.

"Oh my, that song is always hard on my poor little fingers!"

"You played quite well," Jamie said.

"You are too kind," she simpered. "Mama will tell you I practice all the time!"

"Oh indeed! Constantly! The house fairly rings with music!"

"How pleasant that must be."

"Yes, whomever I marry must be a music lover."

"I'm sure he shall be," Jamie said, regretting it instantly as her gaze flashed towards him, and a smile broke out on her face.

She and her mother exchanged glances and he looked uncomfortably at Anne who sat quietly staring at nothing. He cleared his throat and she snapped to attention.

"Excuse my woolgathering."

"Not at all," Jamie said, wishing she would look at him again.

But she kept her gaze averted, leaving him frustrated by the limitations of society. He wanted to go to her, pull her close, and kiss her once more, but there were people about and he could not.

Yet.

Chapter Nine

Anne sat, listening with contempt to her cousin's barely concealed attempts to snare Jamie. Addie was trying so obviously, and that he was doing nothing to escape from it. Though, she reckoned there was little he could actually do besides leave. Her own mind had still not recovered from his kiss, and she did not trust herself to look at him.

She had half a mind to play another song, if only to give her something to do and to silence Addie from flirting with Jamie. Her aunt was only too clearly hinting that her daughter was the perfect wife for a future marquess.

"My dear Adelaide would never put herself forward, but her work with the tenants on the farm is extraordinary. She sews and visits them whenever we stay in the country. Such a tender heart."

Addie did her best to look like the model of a charitable young lady.

Anne rose and went to the piano. She pulled an old favorite out, hoping at least to not discredit herself by playing the song. It was worth it to heard Jamie hush Lady Oglefort as her fingers began to play.

The song was an old Scottish tune of longing, and she knew she played it well, simple as it was. She allowed herself one glance at Jamie while she played, and found her gaze locked onto his, and the message there was so clear her throat constricted and her heart skipped a beat.

She hit a wrong chord and instantly looked down, but not before seeing the contemptuous curve of Addie's mouth. She finished the song and accepted the applause, only to be rushed from the instrument by her cousin's desire to display her superior talent.

Once again, they sat and listened to a performance of more spirit than merit. Her fingers fell with predictable accuracy and a note of aggressiveness, as though playing harder would force the listeners to a higher level of appreciation.

Anne glanced at the clock and decided that the afternoon had lasted long enough. Once Addie finished and curtseyed to the applause, she rose and they all walked to the foyer. Once again, Addie held onto Jamie's arm, though he had done nothing to encourage it. He paused in the foyer and looked at her as he shed himself of Addie.

"Lady Anne, would you do me the honor of accompanying me to my horse?"

Anne's gaze snapped to his, then dropped again and she nodded, walking on ahead of him and out the front door. He followed and carefully shut the door behind them. She reached out to pat Phaeton's cheek and ran her hand down his muscled neck.

"You were always good with animals."

She laughed shortly. "That seems to be about all I am good at."

"Nonsense. I enjoyed your playing. Far more than your cousin's." She glanced up to find him at her shoulder.

"Anne…"

The front door opened and Addie came out. They immediately broke apart. She minced along toward them.

"Could not think what was the matter, dear Anne, you seemed to be lingering and holding Lord Ashton back."

"No. We said what we needed to say and he was just leaving. Good day, Lord Ashton. Thank you for coming."

"The pleasure was all mine." He vaulted aloft and turned Phaeton's head, then rode off at a gallop without looking back.

"Oh, can you imagine what he looks like in his uniform?"

"He looks much the same, I imagine."

"Oh, my dear. If I didn't know how heartbroken you were over Edwin, I would think you and our current Lord Ashton had an understanding."

Anne frowned. "Nonsense. We are old friends, nothing more."

"Oh, I am so glad to hear that. As you might have guessed I find him to be everything tall and manly, so handsome, too."

Jamie, handsome? It had been so long that she had felt her heart flip over every detail of his face that she could no longer judge. He simply looked as he should, and as he did. And she loved him.

Terribly.

That he felt something for her was obvious. But what, exactly? Was he simply trying to step into the shoes he thought his brother had left behind? She did not think so, but she could not know for certain. If only they could talk, but they never seemed to be alone...

She went back into the manor with Addie and the two of them parted ways to go to their respective rooms. Anne let her maid pick something out for the evening as she sat on the window seat looking out. She realized that she had not gone riding since that horrible day and decided that if the morrow was fine, she would ride out.

She leaned her head back and closed her eyes. When next she opened them, her maid was standing beside her, one hand outstretched.

"Oh, miss. You'll need to hurry and dress."

"Oh, Everly, I am so sorry!"

She rose instantly and allowed the maid to undress her then help her into her evening gown. Glancing at her hair, she patted a few tendrils into place and shrugged. It would have to do.

The gong sounded as she stepped free of her room, and she was nearly run over by Lady Oglefort and Addie as they emerged and ran for the dining room. They all entered together, and Lord Welmont looked up from his perusal of the table to nod.

Lady Oglefort enjoyed her supper, and talked consistently throughout. "Oh this is a delicious cream soup, perhaps just a tad thick, but then it clings to the spoon so much neater. Perhaps just a touch more salt…there, that helps. We had such a lovely afternoon with Lord Ashton. Though not so talkative as his brother was. He seems to be one of those quiet, thinking young men."

"He appreciated the music and was very expressive then," Addie said.

"Yes, indeed, he did seem enraptured when you played."

76

"Eh, what? Who's praying?"

Anne cleared her voice and said loudly, "Playing. We had a little musicale this afternoon with Jamie."

Her father pointed his fork at her. "That is Lord Ashton, to you now."

"Yes, sir," she said.

She looked down at her soup, then set her spoon aside and waited for the footmen to clear the soup bowls. Dinner stretched on as Lady Oglefort talked and her father misunderstood. At one point Addie giggled into her pheasant and Anne had to smile. Afterwards they retired to the withdrawing room and were silent. Even Addie's mother seemed to have nothing left to say.

"When do you think we will see Lord Ashton again?" Addie asked.

Anne shook her head. "I don't know. I was thinking of going out riding tomorrow. Would you like to join me?" She immediately regretted her words, for she had intended to check on Elsie while out.

"Unfortunately I did not bring my riding habit. If the carriage were available however…"

"I will definitely be riding. Perhaps we can take out the carriage another day."

Addie stretched a little and covered a yawn. "I am absolutely fatigued. Playing does that to me sometimes…"

"It is the artist in you," said her mother.

Addie preened and rose to go. Her mother was not long after, leaving Anne and her father. He glanced at the clock and looked at her.

"Early hours for those two."

"I am going to join them, Papa."

"Ha! Wore yourself out, did you? Fine then, sleep well."

She kissed him on the cheek, and he waved her away, but he was smiling behind his mustache as he did so. She made her way slowly up the stairs to her room where Everly met her. A short time later she was dressed in her nightgown with a robe wrapped around her for warmth. She sat at her table, excused her maid, and dropped her head down into her hand when the door closed behind her.

Always, always, the thought of Jamie weighed upon her. Fear for his safety if he continued on his naval course. Fear for herself if he should be lost. She did not know how she would go on. There had to be some way to talk him out of continuing on.

He must be made to see that it was folly to continue so!

A doubt crept in. He certainly derived some pleasure from serving, a sort of pride that imbued his demeanor when in his uniform. Certainly there were other titled officers. It was just that Jamie was special. At least to her...

She sighed. At any rate, she would have little opportunity to implore him to leave the navy. Would she if she had the chance? Would she truly try to influence him in any way that went against his conscience?

Part of her screamed that yes, she would. Anything to keep him safe. But then, the sober and reflective part of her reasoned that he must be trusted to know himself and what he was capable of. He had already cheated death once, if anyone knew the risks it was Jamie.

Sighing, she lay down and pulled the covers up

around her. Whether because of her nap or the thoughts running through her head, sleep was a long time coming. When it did come, she was haunted by dreams of explosions and Jamie lying dead.

She sat up, pushed a stray lock of hair from her face and rubbed her eyes. The horror she had felt in her dream lingered in a tightness of her chest and the threat of tears at the back of her eyes. She dragged in a ragged breath and stood to wrap her dressing gown around her before going down to breakfast.

Her father wasn't there, and she had the room to herself. She quickly dished up a plate and poured some tea before sitting down at the table. She stared out the window, which opened onto the west lawn. The sheep her mother had introduced scattered over it. They snatched mouthfuls of grass and chewed them quickly.

She sat for a few minutes longer, enjoying the scene, and then rose finally to go get dressed for her ride. Once in her room, she rang for Everly and pulled out her riding habit. Much as she preferred trousers when riding, she was planning to ride beyond the estate and did not want to subject herself to impertinent remarks.

Sidesaddle it would be. Anne snatched up her riding crop and whisked her skirt out of the way as she went down the stairs. It was a beautiful morning, the clouds having moved off and left but a few scattered remains. She strode to the stables, hoping to brush Angel herself. But when she arrived, she found that had already been done and the saddle was being lowered onto her back.

She fed the bit of carrot she had sneaked from the kitchen to her horse and then climbed up into the saddle. After arranging her skirt, she took the reins and rode off.

It felt good to get away from her cousin's artifice and schemes. That she was playing hard for Jamie was obvious; she had certainly never paid him much mind before Edwin's death. She pushed Angel into a canter and rocked gently along the drive to the main road.

It took the better part of an hour to reach the farm. She found Bessie outside, hanging up washing, though she stopped and shielded her eyes from the sun to look up at Anne.

"Eh, miss! What are you doing here?"

"I just came to check on you and Elsie. Is there anything you need?"

Bessie sniffed and looked away, then shook her head. "No, miss. We were fine before Edwin came into my life; we'll be fine now."

"An-An!"

Elsie reached up for Anne, who picked the little girl up, not minding the smudges of dust and dirt deposited on her skirt by the little feet. Elsie's arms came up to hug her around her neck and loosened her bun slightly. Anne pushed a stray lock that had come loose out of her face and kissed the little cheek.

"What are your plans for Elsie?"

Bessie fondled the tousled curls at her side and shook her head. "Eddie talked about getting married, then said all would be well for her. I never dreamed…" Her voice broke.

"No, no one would."

Anne climbed back onto Angel's back and waved goodbye to the little family. The shadows had lengthened slightly during her visit, and she rode in the sunlight for warmth as much as possible.

As she turned off the little lane that led to the farm, she was surprised to see Jamie astride his horse. They stared at one another.

"What are you doing down this way?"

"Nothing." She shook her head and made to ride past him.

He reached out for her and stopped her with a hand on her arm. "Stay a moment. Something is up. What were you doing?"

She pulled her arm free with more force than she had intended. "Nothing. I'm just out for a ride."

"Meeting someone?"

Her cheeks flamed and she knew he would misinterpret it. Phaeton stopped, then jolted forward until he was level with Angel.

"You were meeting someone. Who?"

"That's really none of your business," she said a little weakly.

Jamie reeled back as though struck, before suddenly spurring his horse into a gallop and riding away.

She shielded her face from the flying dirt and gravel and sighed. Now what? How could she fix this? He obviously felt she had met someone who was the reason for her dirty skirt and mussed hair. Her eyes closed and she let out an explosive breath.

If only he had simply stopped for a moment and talked…

Chapter Ten

Jamie rode hard and fast for nearly a mile before pulling Phaeton up to a jog. He wracked his brain to think of who Anne would be meeting so secretly and what they were doing. He tried to calm himself, but it was useless. He urged Phaeton on again.

Only when his horse was visibly winded did he stop him, and then he was full of contrition. There was no need to drive his horse into the ground because he was upset. *Upset?! Rather more than upset.*

Who was Anne seeing? He could not think. All he knew was his mind was scrambling hard for some hint of who she would prefer to him. And what of Edwin? How long had this been going on?

His motive in seeking her out had been to say goodbye. He had decided that no good would come of his staying at Marrenfort, and that the best thing all around was if he left and returned to the navy. His trunk was being packed even now and he had only to call the carriage 'round to take him to Southampton. He had just received notice that his ship was about to sail within a week. He either needed to show up or resign his commission.

He had decided to sail.

It had not been an easy decision, which was one reason he had sought out Anne. In his heart he had wanted her to dissuade him, to beg him to stay. But she had been involved in an assignation instead…

His fist hit the pommel of his saddle and he breathed out harshly. His mind went over the telltale signs of dirt on her skirt and her slightly mussed hair. Disgust raged through him at the thought of her debasing herself in such a way, but then he chided himself. He did not know to what length the meeting had gone. He slowed his breathing and tried to regain some control.

Still, the sooner he could leave the better.

Marrenfort rose from around the bend in the road and he pushed Phaeton forward the last quarter mile. He swung down, handing the reins off and calling for the carriage before striding toward the manor. Once there he stood in the foyer. Part of him wanted to say goodbye to his father, but then he decided against that. No good would come of talking with him now.

The carriage came around in good time and he supervised the loading of his trunk before climbing in and letting the door close on him. Only then did he sigh and lean back. The morning had not gone as he had hoped.

The drive to Southampton would take two days. But the road was good, and the weather stayed clear so he had no complaints about the travel itself. Just what he had left behind…

****

The two days were tedious. By the time they reached the outskirts of Southampton, his mind had envisioned all kinds of scenarios to explain Anne's red face and appearance. Still, he did not know, and the fact ate at him.

Traffic thickened when they neared the city, and he

felt for his father's carriage driver with all the starts and stops. He smelled the ocean long before they reached it, and gratefully stepped free to stretch and take in the sight of all the ships.

The driver had brought him to the gangplank of *H.M.S. Waynflete* and a pair of seamen came down to help him with his trunk. He saw it stowed when Captain Ellis came up to him saying,

"What's this? You staying on?"

"Yes. If that's all right?"

"That's up to the Admiralty. If they say you stay, who am I to argue. I was just told I might, or might not expect you."

"Well, sir, I am here. What would you have me do?"

"Check on some of the midshipmen. Make sure they are berthed where they should be."

"Aye, sir."

He waved off the carriage and went down to the cockpit of the ship to check on the midshipmen. The ship now held a few new boys, though some were hardly much younger than he was. He remembered his days as midshipman, learning the ropes of the ship so to speak. He had come a long way since then.

The boys stood at attention when he stepped in. He had caught them in a game of cards which were spread out over the table in clusters of hands. He nodded to them, checked their berths were correctly appointed and set up, and then left with another nod. Their voices broke out behind him as he left.

Powder kegs were being loaded as he passed, and he fought a sudden pressure in his head. The powder monkeys ran to and fro, bringing the wooden kegs in from the cart on the quay. He made his way to the wardroom where he and the other lieutenants would mess, and then checked his own berth. He sat for a moment, looking out the window and thinking. They would sail in a day or two, and that would be it. Their mission would be to patrol the Channel and keep it clear of the French who liked to meddle with shipments and harass the British ships.

He was ready to be out at sea again, ready to be away from all the pain of life on land. Still, Anne's face was before him always, and he never seemed to be rid of that particular pain. The stab to his heart every time he thought of her meeting another man in secret…

He blew out a breath as he closed his eyes. He would need to stop thinking about her and learn to focus on the job at hand. Soon they would be under sail, and he would need to be focused indeed.

The clouds had thickened, though the sun still shone between them. He glanced up and hoped it would hold, as sailing in the rain was miserable. Still, as he looked about the ship, he could not but admire the calm efficiency he saw under Captain Ellis's command. Everyone seemed to be doing exactly what they should.

"Hannigan…I mean, Lord Ashton."

"Hannigan is preferred, captain."

"Right then, Hannigan."

The talk became technical as they discussed setting sail on the following day. Jamie listened closely, feeling the old excitement tempered by the dark terror he still felt at the thought of sailing in a warship. He calmed himself and nodded again to Captain Ellis.

"We'll all meet in the wardroom after supper tonight. Everyone should be there."

Jamie returned to his berth. He closed his eyes as thought of Anne intruded on his solitude. He slammed a fist down on the bunk; they really could not get under sail soon enough!

He soon got his wish, for the next morning dawned with plenty of activity for everyone. He supervised the midshipmen in their duties, along with the other lieutenants as the last of the food stores were loaded and a final addition to the officer's mess arrived. Lieutenant James Knight had black hair and flashing dark eyes that hinted at a wicked humor. He clapped Jamie on the shoulder.

"There's two of us Jameses, then, though you're the taller chappie."

"I go by Jamie to my friends," Jamie said.

"And I by Jim. Of course, here we are Hannigan and Knight, and unlikely to be confused with one another!"

Jamie smiled and agreed. Knight was easily shorter by half a foot, but well built.

The mooring lines were eventually thrown off, the sails set, and the ship moved out from the dock and into the deeper water. The ship fairly burst with activity, and time flew by before Jamie had a moment to think about Anne.

It came as the sun set over the sparkling waves of the ocean, and he stood on the main deck looking out, catching a still moment as the ship sailed northward. Somehow the golden sunlight reminded him of Anne, and he took in a deep breath to calm the erratic beat of his heart.

Jamie leaned over the rail and stared down into the water, remembering the explosion and destruction of the *Dorchester*, and the hours spent in the water waiting for rescue. He closed his eyes against the scene and the feelings that followed, wondering if he would ever be free of that fear. How close had the sharks come to getting him that day? He did not know, and did not think he wanted to.

Anne. What could he do about her and this man she was seeing? Was there any hope?

"I know that look," said a voice in his ear.

He started. Jim Knight stood at his elbow, looking out at the sea.

"I don't know what you mean…"

"There's a girl somewhere."

"How did you—"

"I know the look, that's all. Who is she?"

"The girl next door."

"Ah. What's the matter? Don't the family approve?"

"It's a bit complicated."

"Well, try me."

Jamie sighed, thinking. Then he shook his head. "I'm not sure I would do it justice. Maybe another time."

"Of course. They stood at the rail in a companionable silence.

After a moment, Jamie glanced over. "What about you?"

"Me? Was set to be married, but she broke it off. So, off I go again to seek my fortune elsewhere."

"Why did she break it off?"

"She found my lack of material goods a bit harder to cope with than before."

"Ah."

"Yes.," There was a touch of bitterness in his voice, but then he sighed and said more brightly, "So, here we are. Two disappointed gents out to face the world at war. And don't say you aren't crossed in love, for I vow I know that look well enough."

Jamie half-smiled. "I won't deny it."

Jim nodded. "Right then, we know where we stand. Maybe a bit of prize money will change sweet Genevieve's mind."

"You still hope for her, then?"

Jim sighed. "No, not really. But it would feel good to come home victorious."

"I hadn't even thought about the prize money."

"Ah, a man of independent means."

Jamie chuckled. "I suppose you could say that. My father is the Marquess of Marrenfort."

"Ah ha! The picture becomes clearer. And is there a title for my new friend?"

"Lord Ashton, but it is all very new to me."

"Another story, I vow."

"My elder brother was killed. Made me the heir."

"So, why are you here?"

Jamie shrugged and leaned down on his elbows. "Why not? I'm not needed at home, and am useful here. So…the navy."

"I see."

And for some reason Jamie thought he really did. They stood in companionable silence until mess was called when they made their way to the wardroom and sat to eat from the gently rocking table.

That night, lying in his berth, he reflected that he had made a friend and that one fact eased the pain from around his heart. It had felt good to commiserate, however limited. He breathed in deeply and thought perhaps he would be able to endure the next few months at sea.

****

Morning came with a sullen sky. Gray light bled down from a darker mass of clouds onto an even darker sea. The air felt heavy and listless, the sails barely moving and the ship nearly still. Throughout the day the clouds thickened, and the wind picked up as the waves grew to crash against the sides of the ship. Captain Ellis ordered the sails struck and secured so the ship could wait out the coming storm.

Jamie and the other lieutenants scrambled to get their men in position and the task completed. Before the final sail was up, the rain hit, starting with a spatter and ending with sheets that drove against them. It soaked them to the skin within minutes and made the deck slick beneath their feet.

Lightning crashed nearby, and lit the sky up for fragments of a moment. Jamie held onto a rope as they worked to secure the yardarms. The men climbed down from the masts, scuttling below decks to wait out the storm.

A wave crashed over the side and knocked a couple men to their knees. They were up in moments, Jim bracing against a secured lifeboat and hauling one onto his feet. Lightning struck again, illuminating him as he let go of the boat and slipped across the deck. Then another wave hit them, and Jamie fell back.

His feet slipped out from under him as Jim slid past on his way over the side. Jamie grabbed at whatever he could find, hand gripping tight onto the back of Jim's jacket. Jim's legs dangled over the side and he kicked wildly for purchase. Jamie's arm was nearly pulled free of its socket as he struggled to stop Jim from going over.

One of the more gnarled able seamen grabbed a lifeline and slid across the deck to grip Jim beneath his arms. Others hauled them both toward the mast where Jamie reached down to pull Jim to his feet. Another wave crashed over the side, but the men braced for it and the water simply raced past.

"Get below!" shouted the captain and the remaining men trod down the slick stairs and clustered in the wardroom.

Jim reached out a hand to him. "You saved my life tonight, I won't soon forget that."

"Nonsense…" Jamie began, but Jim cut him off.

"You won't convince me otherwise. I was going over. But for you I'd be under the waves now."

Unable to argue the point, Jamie simply clasped the proffered hand and nodded.

****

Morning found them in calmer waters, though the wind still came stiff from the southwest. The sails unfurled and billowed outward as the sun peeked through the iron-gray clouds, pushing the ship hard against the water. They worked the lines to stabilize the rigging until there was a shout from the mizzenmast and the captain trained his spyglass on the distant horizon. Jamie's gaze followed and riveted upon the object.

A ship was there and coming for them.

Chapter Eleven

Anne realized what she must look like with dirty marks over her skirt and her hair loose about her face. "He might at least have let me explain!"

That he had jumped to the wrong conclusion was plain. She rode back to Enniston with her head high and her shoulders rigid with anger. Angel seemed to pick up on her mood, tossed her head, and broke into a trot. She held her back a little, in no rush to get home.

After a few minutes tears smarted her eyes and she dabbed a handkerchief at the corners to prevent them spilling over. *After all, he might have trusted me!*

She wondered where he had gone, and if he had been looking for her. Had he gone to Enniston? Had he seen Addie? She lowered her head and sighed. Likely she would find out as soon as she returned home.

She managed to sneak in and change before her appearance could cause remarks from Addie or her mother. That her maid had questions was evident by the eyebrow that climbed in her forehead. Anne said nothing, simply sat as her hair was straightened and then she rose and took a deep breath to ready herself for Addie.

She twitched her skirt a little, enjoying the feel of the linen against her fingers. It was a newer gown, and she hoped, immune to any snide comments from her fashion conscious cousin.

She found Addie in the drawing room, practicing on the pianoforte and pedantically repeating a section. She broke off as Anne and smiled,

"I take it you got your ride in this morning."

"Yes, and am just now returned. What is that you are practicing."

"An Italian song I found buried in the library. It intrigued me, but I must own to be disappointed."

Anne looked at the sheet. "I'd no idea we had anything like that."

Addie closed the instrument and rose from the seat. "Well, and what shall we do today? Shall we take the carriage over to Marrenfort?"

Anne's eyebrows drew together, and she shook her head. "I saw Jamie this morning out riding. He seemed in a hurry."

Addie lower lip protruded slightly. She wandered over to the settee and sat down rather heavily. Her gaze raked over Anne's gown, and she said with begrudging approval, "I say, Anne, that dress is nice."

"Thank you."

"For the country, of course. It would not do for London."

"Well, we rarely go to London. Papa hates it, can barely be prevailed upon to go to Parliament."

"Do you see your mother often?"

Anne nodded slowly. "I ride out to see her from time to time. She is well."

"Mama can't believe you are still allowed to visit her."

"Well, she is my mother. And really, she did what she believed she had to do."

"But, Anne! To be living unmarried!"

Anne shrugged. "I try not to judge. I don't know what I would have done in her situation." She thought about Jamie, and wondered what she would do for love of him. *Nearly anything.*

She sobered. She was not likely to get the opportunity to test the hypothesis where he was concerned. Feeling the sting of tears once more, she pretended to examine the arrangement of flowers on the side table.

Addie sighed. "Could we ring for tea, do you think?"

"I don't see why not." Anne pulled the bell, then ordered tea be brought to them. She sat back down. "Did Jamie come by this morning, do you know?"

Addie shook her head. "Although, if he came early, I would hardly know. I slept in rather late."

"I hope you slept well."

"Well enough. What shall we do today?"

"I suppose we can take the carriage out for a drive into Brumley. The haberdasher there is quite nice."

Addie sighed. "I suppose so." She paused, then added, "I don't suppose we could have a ball…?"

Anne considered the time left to them. "Perhaps we could have a few couples over for supper and a little dancing. Nothing so formal as a ball."

"Oh, yes, Anne! Please let's do! Who shall we invite?"

She named a few names and smiled at Addie's blank approval.

"I will speak with the housekeeper and then we can send out the invitations today. Perhaps a week hence."

Addie all but clapped her hands. "I have just the dress to wear! I can't wait to show you!"

Just then the footman brought the tea tray in and set it beside Anne. She poured a cup and dropped three sugars into it before handing it to Addie, then poured another for herself. Though she usually drank it with one sugar and a splash of milk, this time she drank it black, the way Jamie preferred, her mind going to him and wondering what it would be like to dance with him…if he even agreed to come. It had been so long since she had danced with Jamie…

They finished their cups. Addie dragged Anne up to her room and sorted through the dresses in the wardrobe before pulling one out. She held it up to herself and spun around before stopping so Anne could see it.

It shimmered in the sunlight, pale gold sheer over white silk. Golden roses had been embroidered over it and it was gathered at the bust. Tiny threads arranged around the puffs at the shoulders caught the light. Anne was awestruck.

"It's lovely!"

"Is that all you can say?"

"Yes, it is. I'm speechless."

Addie smiled, satisfied. "It is quite new. I haven't worn it yet, besides trying it on of course. And look at the slippers I have to wear with it." She set the dress down and pulled out a pair of white shoes with gold embroidered around the top and a golden silk rose attached.

Lady Oglefort came in and stopped at the sight that met her eyes. "Dearest, whatever are you doing?"

"Anne and I are planning a dance and I was showing her my newest gown."

"Ah! Well that all sounds splendid. When is this to

be?"

"A week or so, I believe. I need to consult with Papa and Stevens the housekeeper."

"Well go, go, let us know when it is to be so we can plan!" Anne was practically shooed from the room and paused just outside the door. Eyebrows up, she went in search of her father. She found him out in the garden, discussing something with the head gardener.

"I tell you I see bugs on my great-grandmother's roses. They must be dealt with."

"Aye, sir, we know. We are treatin' 'em," said Jones in his usual hoarse whisper.

"Threatening? Yes, I should think they are threatening the roses."

"Papa, he said they know and are treating them."

The gardener used her appearance as an opportunity to escape.

Anne raised her voice again. "Which roses are affected?"

He spent several minutes showing her and had calmed somewhat before she asked, "Papa, have you any plans for the evening of Tuesday next?

"Tuesday next…Tuesday next… No, can't say that I do. Wednesday I am shooting with Hershey and Pault." He named two old friends from a nearby town.

She explained about the dance, and he beamed.

"Wonderful, wonderful! Just the thing for you girls! Especially now that the Hannigan boy has gone off to the navy again."

"Wait, what was that?"

"Lord Ashton returned to war, just this morning."

Fear clutched at her chest and closed off her throat. Jamie gone? Already? Before she could even say goodbye? And thinking that she…

Oh Lord, what did he think of her?

She sat on the stone bench and struggled to get control of herself. Jamie had been out to see her, to say goodbye, and had found her looking tousled and dirty. He had jumped to a conclusion and raced off…to war.

To war.

The weight of it pressed down on her and her hand clenched at her chest. Somehow, she had to find a way to make this right. Could she write to him? What would she say? What needed to be said, had to be said in person. She dragged a breath in, and then another. She could do nothing for now. He would come home, he had to. And then they would have a conversation.

She walked back to the house, hoping she could get past Addie without being caught. Addie pounced on her the moment she entered.

"And? Yes?"

"It is fine with Papa. Let's talk with Stevens and then we can send the invitations."

Addie linked her arm through Anne's and followed her down to the housekeeper's room below stairs. The dour Mrs. Stevens greeted them and heard all Anne had to say.

"Aye, miss. We'll 'andle it."

Addie squealed and jumped a little. Then she pulled her back up the stairs where they spent the rest of the afternoon writing out invitations and addressing them. Finally, as the sun was setting behind Enniston, they were sent out.

Addie was in high spirits. She chattered happily through supper, planning the music, the dances, and even suggesting ideas for the menu. Anne nodded, rarely offering anything of her own. Finally, Addie seemed to wind down and frowned at Anne.

"You are very quiet this evening."

"I'm sorry, just thinking I guess."

"What shall we do tomorrow?"

Anne pushed a green bean around her plate with her fork, then set it down and straightened. "I thought we could take a picnic to the folly."

Addie's mouth opened in an 'O' and her eyes flashed. "I shall wear my blue-sprigged muslin and my newest bonnet."

"That sounds lovely."

"What shall you wear?"

Anne could hardly remember what dresses she had at the moment. Her head was full of Jamie and the danger he was going toward. Desperately she hunted through her memory for an appropriate gown.

"Umm...my muslin with the pink rosettes."

"Ohhh, that sounds rather nice. We will be quite the pair. Where is the folly?"

"Marrenfort."

"Perhaps we could invite Lord Ashton."

"No, he's returned to the navy." Anne's voice caught and she took a sip of wine.

"Oh, well, that's rotten luck."

"Adelaide, language," said Lady Oglefort.

"Well, Mama, it is."

"There will be other nice young men at the dance next week."

"Yes, I suppose."

Anne picked up her spoon to try and force down the strawberry ice that had been placed before her. It froze her tongue and palate, leading to a headache. She set the spoon down again and made a face.

Addie chuckled. "You need to let it melt on your tongue first."

"Mmm, well luckily Cook doesn't make them often," Anne said.

"Our cook never does, and I do so love them."

"Our cook tends to favor trifle," Lady Oglefort said.

"Jellies," Anne said.

"Ah."

"Mama, we are taking a picnic to a folly at Marrenfort tomorrow."

"That sounds lovely, dearest."

Supper finished finally and Anne retired to her room where she could be alone for the night and think. Jamie would be in an inn by now, and reach his ship the next day. She wondered if he thought of her at all. Then worried about what he would be thinking of her.

Her maid came in and helped her out of her clothes and into a nightdress. She gathered up the dress and shoes to brush and clean, leaving Anne sitting at the dressing table, staring at the candle.

After carrying it to her bed, she set it on the nightstand and laid down, watching the flame dance in the invisible current. Her nurse had once frightened her with stories of ghosts who played with the flames, and she remembered the old fear she had once felt when candle flames moved. It was her mother who had calmed her then, and she found herself missing her suddenly. Somehow, she thought her mother would understand.

The next day was rainy, and all plans for the folly were put on hold. Anne read and Addie practiced piano.

They played cards and embroidered. Throughout the day acceptances for the dance arrived and were a point of glee for Addie.

The sun rose intermittently through the clouds on the following day and Anne called the carriage to take them to the folly. As promised, Addie wore her blue-sprigged muslin and Anne remembered to wear her pink rosebud muslin. The kitchen had prepared a large basket for them, and a servant came with them to spread the blanket on the ground and serve the food for them.

Anne stepped out of the carriage and waited for Addie to join her. The folly sat on a little hill, looking down through a break in the trees toward Marrenfort. Gypsy's Gate was just visible in the breach and Anne shuddered, memories of that horrible day flooding back. Addie seemed to notice her paleness.

"Is that where…"

"Yes."

Addie stared at the old gate, overgrown with vines and brambles. "Strange to think that it will forever be associated with Edwin's death."

"Yes."

Anne turned from the view and walked into the little temple. A statue of Athena stood within, and both girls considered her for a moment before Addie asked, "Why her, do you think?"

"Well, the marchioness was a great reader, and Athena is the goddess of wisdom. So, there you are."

"Hmph. Aphrodite would be more to my liking. Or Eros!" She giggled and Anne felt her cheeks grow warm. Addie swung around and went to one of the columns to look out at Marrenfort. "Such a handsome estate. I can't think why you aren't trying for it."

"Edwin…"

"Oh, of course! I am sorry. It's just, the new Lord Ashton is much more to my liking. Tall, dark… well, a little, and quiet. One is always wondering what he is thinking."

"He is a deep one."

"That's just it; he's deep. But, I think someone like me could snap him out of it somewhat."

Anne stepped over the damp ground to where the blankets had been spread on the floor of the folly. "The grass is still too wet, so we shall have to sit here."

Addie lowered herself carefully. The food was unpacked and a filled plate passed to her. Anne accepted her own and sat, considering Marrenfort. It was an impressive house, solid and Elizabethan, rather prone to ramble in its wings, unlike Enniston all boxed up and square. She had always liked it, but had never had any sights set on it as a home. With a shock she realized that Jamie would one day inherit the estate. She had not thought of it before now.

"I shall be doing the Season again this year. It was great fun at first, quite awful by the end. I am not looking forward to it this time. I'd much rather Lord Ashton came home and whisked me off to Marrenfort."

"Well, he's not likely to do so any time soon. There's a war on."

"Oh yes, I'd heard. Something to do with the Americans."

"And the French, yes."

"Papa talks on and on about politics and such. It is so tedious."

"Father mostly thinks about his roses and

shooting."

"What does he think of your mother?"

"We don't discuss it."

"No, I can imagine not. I wonder if he is still angry about it all. It's been nearly two years now, hasn't it?"

Anne simply took another sip of her tea. She stared at the leaves in the bottom of her cup and then set it aside. She hated that she could not think of something distracting to say to change the subject; her mind had simply seized upon it instead.

"It was quite the talk of the town when it happened, until Sylvia Delvine ran off with Lord Gorman and they were discovered weeks later living in London. Her father took her back in but no one has seen her since. I had heard there was a baby, but no one can confirm that."

Anne felt nothing but sympathy for Sylvia Delvine, whoever she was.

They lapsed into a silence, then Addie sighed and leaned back on her elbows to look out over the vista.

"Mmm. It is so peaceful here. How lovely for you to be able to visit like this."

"Lord Marrenfort is most gracious."

"Tell me, Anne, what did you really think about Edwin?"

Anne's throat constricted and she tried to clear it. "I admired him, of course. Everyone did. He was just so full of life, doing things the way he wanted them done without any hindrance of others' opinions."

"The perfect rake!"

"He was no rake!" Anne's voice sounded harsh to her own ears and Addie shot her a glance.

"Well pardon me, I did not know him so well. But,

one did hear things…"

"What on Earth could you have heard to Edwin's detriment?"

"Just that he was a terrible flirt, but an excellent dancer. I only danced with him the once, but I thought he was rather good."

"I see. So nothing, really, except that he was a flirt."

"In some circles that is enough," Addie said.

Anne pushed herself up from the ground. "I'm going to take a turn. I shall be back."

She was off before Addie could jump up to join her. She went straight to the back of the folly and struggled for a moment to gain some composure. The proximity to Gypsy's Gate and Addie's blithe mention of Edwin had started a sequence of emotions she was unable to master immediately. A couple deep breaths helped, and she continued on her way. She startled a small flock of sheep who scattered into the trees on the side of the hill.

Addie was sitting in the carriage when she came around the side of the folly. The picnic materials were being packed up and Anne allowed herself to be helped into the carriage. Addie sat turned slightly away, and Anne divined that she was out of sorts with her. Unwilling to break the silence, Anne simply sat on the opposite seat and looked out the window.

A sense of impending doom came over her.

Chapter Twelve

The ship approached, sails out and racing toward them. Stuns'ls, the auxiliary sails used for speed, were out on either side of the main and topsails, making the ship look huge as she moved silently forward.

"All hands to battle stations!" Captain Ellis yelled.

The *H.M.S. Waynflete* burst into activity. The deck below rumbled with the weight of cannon being pushed into place. Powder monkeys scrambled to get the powder for their assigned cannons and men struggled under the weight of the ball to be loaded in the cannon muzzle.

The *Waynflete* yawed, bringing her broadside guns within range of the French ship which shot her fore cannon. One ball ricocheted off the hull of the *Waynflete*, glancing off and splashing into the sea. By that point, the *Waynflete*'s cannon were ordered to fire, and it let loose a resounding volley as the balls sang through the air, hitting wood and water alike.

Cries broke out on the other ship, but she had finished swinging around by then and shot her own complement of cannon off toward the *Waynflete*. She was close enough for Jamie to read her name. *Vierge*. Her cannon were aimed high, and the balls tore through the sails and crashed onto the deck. The *Waynflete*'s cannons were ready, and they answered.

Vierge's hull thundered as cannon balls crashed

into it, two breaking through with a splintering sound. Cries and screams from within the ship echoed within and a new flurry of activity appeared. *Vierge* yawed around, the wind pushing her closer to *Waynflete* as she let loose another volley of cannon fire.

Waynflete's sides echoed and splintered as the balls hit. Sails ripped as balls went through them. One sailor was hit and thrown overboard, dead before he hit the water. Blood blossomed where the body fell, then dissipated away. Jamie steadied his breathing and quickly readied his gun and sighted a man on the other ship, firing as *Waynflete* let her cannon fly, filling the air with acrid smoke.

The *Vierge*'s mizzenmast snapped with a sharp crack and a cheer went up on the *Waynflete*. But now the ships were within boarding range, and Jamie quickly reloaded his gun as the French prepared to try and board the English ship. He picked off yet another uniformed man and set to reloading.

Something crashed into him, throwing him backward to the ground and snatching his breath. Searing pain followed, and his hand came away bloody from his chest. Blood spread outward from the gunshot wound over his right breast. Jim was suddenly there, hooking his arms under his and pulling him backward out of the fray. He opened a door and pulled him into the relative quiet of the captain's rooms.

"Lie still, I'll be back in a moment."

Jamie laid back, his chest filling with blood and making it difficult to breathe. He coughed, pain shooting through his chest and blood bubbling out of his mouth. He rolled onto his injured side to give his good lung a chance to fill with air and continued to struggle to breath.

Outside shots rang, cannon resounded, and now and then a thud hit the ground as a man fell in the fight. Something crashed against the door and the latch rattled. A gunshot rang out followed by a thud and a scraping sound.

Silence fell, eerie and punctuated by small sounds he could not identify. Had they won? Were they now prisoners? He did not know, only that each breath was a struggle and brought new waves of crippling pain.

More scraping, sliding sounds came from outside the cabin and suddenly Jim was there, kneeling down beside him. He had a slash through the sleeve of his coat and a smear of blood down his breeches, but seemed whole. He bent to peer closely at Jamie.

"Still breathing, that is excellent!"

"Did we win?" Jamie gasped.

"Yes, they surrendered. But the surgeon is busy. I'll go tell him about you. Lie still and just keep breathing."

Eyes screwed shut in pain, Jamie nodded and continued to breathe shallow and fast. Jim was gone for several minutes before he returned with the ship's surgeon, who knelt and examined him with quick, deft fingers. His jacket was peeled back from him, and then his shirt was cut away and stripped off his chest. Looking down, his vision swam as blood bubbled forth from a small, neat hole.

"That's where it went in; let's see if it came out."

Jamie was gently turned over. He coughed up more foamy blood which Jim mopped up with his own neckerchief.

The doctor grunted. "Bullet is lodged beside a rib.

I'll have to dig it out."

"What?" Jamie gasped.

But the surgeon reached into his bag and pulled out a knife which he plunged confidently into Jamie's flesh.

He gritted his teeth together as the knife explored his back for a moment before the doctor grunted again and pulled his hand back. Jamie struggled to focus on the object now held before his eyes. A drop of blood dripped before it was whisked away, and it clinked into a metal tray.

"Now, your right lung is torn through. You're going to be coughing up blood and worse for a while. You must lay on your right side to give your left lung the best chance for breathing and so you don't bleed into it. I'll bind you up, but you'll need to fight."

"Where shall we take him?"

"Leave him here. Make him a pallet and move him carefully onto that. Hopefully the captain won't mind."

"What is going on here?" The captain burst in, and the surgeon stood to face him.

"Hannigan here took a ball to the chest. He mustn't be moved."

There was a moment of silence.

"We'll make him comfortable. If you're finished here, there are more men who need you."

The doctor's case snapped shut and lifted out of Jamie's sight. The surgeon's footsteps receded. Captain Ellis went to a trunk, pulled out several blankets, and folded them into a pallet near the wall. Then he and Jim carefully moved Jamie inch by inch until they were able to lift him onto it.

Jamie coughed again, and Jim wiped the foamy blood from his lips. He gasped,

"Thank you."

"Not a thing," Jim said.

Captain Ellis left without a word and Jim hovered until Jamie said, "Go help them, I'm fine."

Jim clapped him gently on the shoulder and walked off with a single backward look. Panic rose in him at being alone, as though the solitude could entice him away from life. He mentally shook himself and brought the cloth Jim had given him up to his mouth as he coughed again.

Time seemed to have slipped when he next opened his eyes. There was no light, and for a moment he thought he had been sealed in a coffin, but he made out shapes in the darkness and realized it was only night. As though sensing that he had awakened, Jim entered carrying a candle and set it on the floor beside Jamie.

"Still alive, I see."

"Only just."

"It's enough. You'll have a rough go of it before we get you back to England."

"Is that where we're headed?"

"Yes, taking the *Vierge* back. Denniston is commanding her."

"Good man, he'll do well. How many did we lose?"

"Seven, with three more uncertain. Nine others wounded but expected to live. That's not counting the French."

"How long before we're home?"

"A week. You should be through the worst of it by then."

"Thanks for pulling me out of the fray."

"Thanks for stopping me going over the side."

They were silent for a moment, then Jamie asked, "Can I get something to drink?"

Jim left for a few minutes, and returned with a mug. He held it to Jamie's lips, and he drank a few sips of the broth it contained.

"That was from supper. Fish stew."

"It tastes good. I needed something." He glanced around. "Where's the captain?"

"He's still overseeing everything. Not likely to leave the deck until we know the outcome of some of the injured."

"Good captain."

Jim yawned and Jamie sighed. "What time is it?"

"After ten…"

"Get yourself to bed. I'll be fine."

"The doctor mentioned infection."

"Well, it won't take me in the next few hours."

Jim yawned again and left. Jamie was alone in the semi-darkness with only a single candle to provide light. He struggled to lift his head enough to drink another sip of the broth. Then he set it down and laid his head back on the pillow.

When next he opened his eyes it was to see light streaming in through the captain's windows and the candle burned down to a nub. The tumbled blankets showed that Captain Ellis had finally retired the night before from his vigil. Jamie tried to push himself up, His chest spasmed as a shock of pain shot through him.

Gasping, he laid down, then coughed up more blood. The blankets moved, and Captain Ellis rose up and came to him.

"You all right, son?"

"Just tried to get up," croaked Jamie.

"None of that. You're bedbound for the remainder of this trip I would say. We'll take care of you."

Jamie nodded and rolled slowly onto his back. The movement caused pain, but also felt good for a moment. He lay there breathing quietly as the captain moved around his cabin, getting dressed and washing his face in the basin. When next Jamie opened his eyes, it was to see Jim kneeling there beside him.

"Made it through the night, I see."

"Yes, thanks to you. Where's the captain?"

"He had his three hours of sleep, now he's off to check on the crew and the ships. How's the chest?"

"Not coughing up so much blood, but the pain…"

"I'll see if the doctor has any laudanum. I should think you would warrant some."

"God, yes…"

"I'll be back, then. Anything else?"

"Something to drink?"

Jim smiled. "Just a minute."

He left, leaving the door open so the sounds from the bustle of the crew working the ship filtered within. Fresh air buffeted around him as the door opened, and he tried not to breathe too deeply. Steps sounded and he recognized the doctor's efficient pace. The bag dropped into place beside him, and he looked up.

The doctor was measuring a reddish-brown liquid into a small cup which he then held up to Jamie's mouth. "Here, lad, drink this down and you will feel better."

Jamie choked a little on the bitter taste but managed to get it down. He leaned back and waited for the medicine to work. Jim arrived with some water and Jamie had once more to raise up slightly to drink.

109

Though stale, the water helped wash the bitterness of the laudanum away.

Soon a rush of warmth that overlaid the pain went through him and lifted his spirits. Jim smiled and left, promising to return. Jamie simply nodded and fell back into a medicated stupor. Time swirled by in a sequence of disconnected events as boots appeared and left, hands reached for him; someone washed his face and changed the bandage around his chest.

Afternoon shadows had spread throughout the cabin by the time the laudanum's effects had worn off. Jamie took a deep breath and swore to himself that he preferred the pain of his injury to the stupor of the laudanum.

Jim arrived, lowered himself to the ground and said, "Ah, you're back I see."

"I think so. God… never again."

"And just think, there are people addicted to that."

"I can't think why."

"Well, we are a few days out from Southampton. The *Vierge* is right behind us under our command, of course."

"Slow going?"

"A little, but not too bad. We'll get there and get you home."

"That's the plan, is it?"

"Yes. Rent a cart and get you back to Marten Manor."

"Marrenfort."

"Right. Your family will be happy to see you."

"I wouldn't be so sure about that. Mother is gone, brother is gone, only Father left and he will find my presence irksome."

Jim frowned in disbelief. "Surely not."

Jamie simply stared up at the beams that made up the ceiling. "I'm not feeling too well, Side effect of the laudanum?"

Jim laid a cool hand on his forehead. "You're warm to the touch. I'll get the doctor."

He returned within moments, doctor in tow. Jamie was examined once again and finally the doctor leaned back.

"Fever. Inevitable, really. Redness around the wounds. We'll keep you cool and clean; that's all we can do. And hydrated."

"I'll look after him," Jim said.

"Good man." He packed up his kit and left, leaving them alone.

Jamie reached for the cup of water and drank before leaning back painfully once more.

"I need to go check on some things. I'll be back."

Jamie simply nodded, brow furrowed in intensifying pain. He shivered a little, and wracking pain shot through him.

It felt suddenly cold...

Chapter Thirteen

Anne looked herself over in the mirror. Her lavender gown reflected the candlelight in smooth swathes of gold. She touched a hand to her hair, curled and arranged to look like Athena herself. She sighed to think that Jamie would not see her.

She wondered again where he was and whether he was safe. Pausing for a moment before heading out of her room, she tried to get control of her thoughts and feelings so as to get through the night.

The small ballroom had been cleared of all furniture to make room for the seven couples dancing. She went to the foyer to greet everyone as they arrived and noted that Addie and her mother were already there.

Addie looked resplendent in her golden gown. A pang of envy shot through Anne at the thought of having such a dress. She went up to her cousin and said,

"Oh my, you look lovely!"

"Thank you, and you look quite nice, too! Oh, how I wish Lord Ashton were going to be here."

"Yes, that would have made it complete. But here are some other friends we can spend the evening with." She greeted a tall, young man, rather spotty, who quite clearly was struck with Addie at first glance. He asked to escort her to the room, and Addie grudgingly accepted. Anne watched them go, then turned to meet the next family of young women. They were a loud, happy family and infused the evening with a bit of life by their mere presence. Next came another young man who was dark and rather studious looking. He apparently knew the family of young ladies for they instantly absorbed him into their midst.

Anne's face ached from smiling, the more so because she was filled with sadness at Jamie's absence and worry for his safety. And still people came...

Her father had given up trying to hear anything anyone said and simply nodded and grunted things like, "Pleased to have you," and "Nice to see you again." Anne took the moments in between the arrivals to shout their names into his ear as a reminder.

Finally, everyone appeared to be present. The room was filled with the sounds of talking and the buzz of people mingling. The quartet announced a dance and couples assembled, Addie with another young man, this one blond and rather haughty. Anne found herself applied to and accepted the tall, spotty youth.

He danced well, and she remembered he was the Honorable Charles Jarrett. His family had an estate near the next town to the east. She wracked her brain to remember something about him, but failed.

"I know we have met before, but I can't remember when or where."

He smiled. "We met at the Campbells' some two years ago. They had a weekend party, and you came with your mother."

"Ah, yes." That had been just before her mother's announcement, and she had been distracted by her mother's distant moods.

"Are you quite well, Lady Anne?"

"Indeed, yes. It has just been so long since I danced that I am finding it fatigues me. Still, I would not stop for the world."

"Ah yes, I can see how that would be. Young ladies are not sportsmen as young men are expected to be."

"No, but we are supposed to stand more than a single dance!"

He smiled and spun her around deftly, then the music faded and she thanked him. Going in search of the punch, she passed Addie preening in front of the family of young ladies—the Yardleys—and suppressed a smile. Someone, at least, was enjoying herself.

The evening flowed slowly along, dance after dance. Anne spent some time with the Yardleys and found them to be four plain, but happy young women, quite close in age. She found it difficult to tell them all apart, so similar in appearance were they. As an only child, she rather envied their closeness and thought how comforting it would be at times.

One of them, Lavinia, asked, "Do you not find it lonely at times being the sole child in a family?"

"I do, at times. But I also enjoy a certain amount of solitude."

"Solitude!" cried Lydia, "None of us knows anything about that. I don't believe I have spent ten minutes alone since the day I was born!"

Her sisters agreed with her, and yet Anne noted they were quite good-natured about it. "I guess we are all used to what we are used to, then."

After leaving the Yardleys, she went in search of Addie who was engaged in conversation with young Lord Walter Hampden. Lord Walter was avidly listening to Addie as she recounted a disastrous carriage ride in London.

"And then the cab, or hansom, or whatever they are called crashed into the side of our carriage and cracked the varnish, and yet he yelled at our driver as though it were our fault. Our wheel came off not long after and Father declared it because of being struck in the side like that."

"I had not heard this story," Anne said.

"Oh, well. There has been so much else to talk about."

Anne suspected the story had belonged to another individual. Addie was simply repeating it for Lord Walter's enjoyment and as a way to get attention. She let it go and wove in and amongst the other groups until the little ball began to break up in the early hours of the morning.

She climbed gratefully into bed that night, thankful it was over, and thinking once more of Jamie before falling asleep.

****

Rain spattered down for the third day in a row, as Anne sighed. The only good thing was that Addie and her mother were leaving today, and Anne could finally look forward to having her home to herself.

She waited in the foyer as they gathered themselves together, accepting the basket filled with cold chicken, bread, and the like from the kitchen. Addie made a great show of kissing Anne as they walked down to the carriage underneath the umbrella held by a footman. They were handed within, and the door was shut. After a moment, the carriage rolled away.

Anne sighed, the burden of having her cousin for over two weeks now finally over. She wandered listlessly about the house, mentally reclaiming it. The pianoforte sat in its accustomed corner of the drawing room, and she sat at it for a while, playing an old song she had known most of her life. Somehow, though, it made her think of her mother and she paused.

Staring out at the interminable rain, she wished for a moment to be with her. She would even stomach the company of Havers if it meant leaning one more time on her mother's shoulder. But short of calling her own carriage to take her into Brumley, there would be no visit that day.

She wondered how Jamie was faring, and if he'd had to face any storms at sea. A nagging worry lay behind her thoughts of him, and it was all she could do not to clench her fists in frustration.

After shutting the instrument, she pushed up from the seat and went to the window where water droplets chased each other down the panes. A voice sounded behind her and she started.

"Another day of this and I fear for the roses." Her father's voice sounded querulous.

"The rose beds drain well, Father, I shouldn't worry."

Lord Welmont came to stand beside her and stared out in the direction of the gardens. "I tell myself that they have survived everything the world has thrown at them for these decades, and yet worry that the next thing that comes along will be their undoing."

"But then what, Father? We plant more roses."

"And yet I will have let down the estate. It won't be passed on whole as it came to me."

"I'm sure Richard will not mind the loss of a few roses." He was a distant cousin who was set to inherit upon Lord Welmont's death.

"Speaking of Richard, he writes that he wishes to visit in a week. Have we any reason to say no?"

"None that I can think of. How long does he plan to stay?"

"He did not say, but I imagine at least a fortnight."

"I suppose we must have him."

"Yes, my dear, nothing to be done about it. Besides, you have always done well together."

Anne was silent. Richard had great admiration for himself, and was usually anxious that others acknowledge his superior traits. Perhaps ten years older than Anne, he had never married, something that bothered Lord Welmont no end.

"Be good to have him about for a change. Perhaps we will go shooting."

"He likes to hunt."

"Perhaps not this time."

"No."

Lord Welmont trooped away in his characteristic, straight-legged manner and Anne left the window to wander through the hall with its enormous picture frames encapsulating the painted figures of distant relatives. She knew them all, from the second Lady Welmont in her elaborate gown and little dog, to her father's coming of age portrait where he stood very straight, with an uncertain air. Family, portrayed in their finest and at their best. Family in real life was something quite different.

And still it rained.

And now Richard was coming. Where was Jamie?

Was he safe? She knew he did not like her cousin, and she was inclined to agree with him. She had read once about an octopus with tentacles that clung with sucker-like disks. This, she thought, was what Richard was like, wet and clingy.

Her father's step echoed in the hall and his voice addressed the butler. Posting a letter to Richard, she guessed. She found herself by another window, looking out at the dismal day.

She drew her shawl close about her shoulders to ward off the cold coming from the glass.

****

It was a week later when Sir Richard arrived. He came on horseback with his trunk in a cart joined by his valet. He dropped down and instantly came to Anne to grasp her hand in his and kiss it fervently.

"My dear cousin, delighted to see you again!"

"Thank you, Richard."

He pulled her hand onto his elbow and walked toward the house. "How is your father?"

"He is well. I expected him here to greet you, but something must have happened."

He dropped his voice. "And your mother, how is she?"

In a normal voice Anne replied, "She is well, keeping busy and hearty."

"Good, good. I am glad. She was always most gracious to me. No hint whatsoever that…well, erm…"

Anne disentangled herself from him and led the way up the staircase toward the north wing where his room lay. After opening the second door on the right she preceded him and stood to let him take in his surroundings.

"Is this the haunted room?"

"Do you believe in ghosts, Sir Richard?"

"I am not sure. Which one is supposed to haunt this room?"

"The Gray Man. We believe it is the third Lord Welmont, but no one is sure. He did die in this room, but then I suppose many people have."

"Yes, that is the thing about old houses, hard to find a bed no one has died in."

"Or been born in."

"Or conceived…" He shot her a look that caused her insides to squirm and she moved toward the door.

"I hope you will be most comfortable."

Anne hurried out to her own room where she shut the door firmly behind her. She unconsciously brushed herself off as though to rid herself of the lingering threads of Richard's presence. She lay down on her bed and wondered why talk of death had brought Jamie to mind.

They had not heard of any battles on the sea, but then they would not for some time. And news of Jamie must go first to Marrenfort and the marquess. Who knew how long before she found out? She wondered how impertinent it would be to ride over and simply ask.

But how to escape Richard first? The man loved to ride, so even that release was more difficult for her. She blew out a breath in frustration and frowned at the canopy. What to do? She could hardly walk over to Marrenfort, especially in all the mud following the rain. Perhaps if she woke before dawn and arrived at far too early an hour for calling.

"Ugh. I shall just have to watch for a chance to get

away."

She picked up a shawl and went downstairs. She made her way into the drawing room and sat down at the piano to play a light tune. Anne was halfway through when a movement caught her eye and she looked up.

And saw Richard.

He stood leaning against the wall, watching her. He smiled and moved to the decanter to pour himself a brandy. He observed her over the rim of the glass as he sipped.

"Very lovely."

"Thank you."

"I set a great store by music."

"I should think almost everyone does."

"You would be surprised at the number of wretches who exist without a proper appreciation of music."

Anne could think of nothing to say to this. She closed the instrument and rose from the seat to leave the room, but Richard forestalled her,

"Don't go! I came especially to see you."

"Well, I haven't changed all that much. Still just Anne."

"Isn't that enough?"

"I suppose it depends upon whom you ask."

"I'm sure anyone who knows you would be quite satisfied with who you are."

Anne looked helplessly around. He loomed over her, and her skin crawled. *Strange, he is no taller than Jamie, and yet so much more foreboding.* She lowered herself into a chair and clasped her hands trying not to twine her fingers.

He set down the glass and sat as well, facing her,

his dark gaze seeming to bore into hers. She tried to look everywhere but at him. "You haven't ridden out since you arrived."

"I was hoping you would join me."

"I am not inclined to ride."

"Pity. Can I not persuade you?"

"I don't know, I had thought to write some letters and finish some sewing." Her mind flew desperately to anything but riding with him.

"Ah, well, far be it from me to intrude on such domestic arts."

"I don't know how artistic I am at either, only that they need to be done."

She rose then and nodded to him, before walking swiftly from the room and heading quickly up the stairs. Once back in her room, Anne leaned against the door and wondered why she felt as though she had just escaped from danger.

She dug out her sewing and sat on the chaise beside the window, preferring to stay in her room than go down and be haunted by Richard. She finished repairing the hem of her father's shirt, something that could have been done by anyone, but that she actually enjoyed doing. She sighed. Some days there was not enough with which to fill up the day. Especially now that she so desperately wished to stay occupied and beyond reach.

The flowers in the vestibule needed redoing. Perhaps if she slipped downstairs she could go out to the gardens while the rain had stopped and cut some late flowers. Anne pulled on one of her older pelisses and buttoned it up, then crept downstairs to one of the rooms where they kept the gardening supplies. Her gloves and a pair of secateurs, along with a basket, were all she needed.

The sky was still gray, and the air was damp and cold. It clung to her and soon chilled her as she made her way from flower bed to flower bed. Soon she had a good assortment of flowers with which to do an arrangement and made her way back indoors.

A pleasant hour passed as she placed the stems in the frog, clipping and adjusting from time to time. Soon enough it was done, and Anne turned, only to drop her basket in surprise to find Richard standing behind her!

He bent quickly to pick up the basket and handed it to her. "I am so sorry. I did not mean to startle you."

"How long have you been there?"

"Only a few minutes. I did not want to disturb you."

She patted her beating heart and took in a deep breath. "You are as silent as a ghost, Sir Richard."

"I've told you to call me Richard."

"It is so difficult to unlearn a lifetime of habit."

"Your lifetime is not so long as to make it so difficult."

She gave the barest of smiles, but said only, "If you will excuse me, I need to return the tools and the basket."

"I'll come with you." He lifted the basket and motioned her on ahead.

Unable to find an excuse to escape, she led the way. Once the tools and the basket were stowed in their spot, he pulled her hand through the crook of his arm and headed out into the garden.

"I believe your grandfather did much work on the layout of these beds."

She tried to yank her hand back, but he laid his own over the top and she was trapped.

"Yes, yes he did."

"I have always thought them well arranged and stocked. I might one day plant some new hybrid roses. Would you approve of that?"

Anne frowned. This was not at all pleasant talk to her. "It will be beyond my ability to approve of anything you do with Enniston."

"Meaning you would not approve of anything I do?"

"No, meaning that it will be yours. I will be long gone to another home."

"I would not have you believe you will be banished the moment your father passes on."

"I don't care to think about that." She determinedly pulled her hand back and clasped both in front of her.

"I simply mean to say you need not have fear of losing your home on that day. Indeed, one might say you have within your means the ability to retain the very home you might lose."

Luckily, they had reached the stairs by then, and Lord Welmont was just coming out of the library.

"Ah, Sir Richard! I have been looking for you! I have found a new ledger which I wanted to show you."

"Of course."

Richard's gaze tried to bore into hers, but she steadfastly avoided it and made her way into the drawing room. She waited until their voices receded and sat down beside the harp. She plucked a few strings, then tried one of the songs she had learned while younger, But her fingers grew sore and she was forced to abandon it.

Feeling suddenly trapped, she went to the window and pressed her forehead against the cold glass. Her breath flared onto it, and she thought of Jamie out on the open sea. The old fear gripped her. She had to know how he was, and the only place she could find that out was at Marrenfort.

Anne trotted up the stairs to her room, changed quickly into her riding habit and then headed downstairs toward the stable. Her horse stood in her box, dozing placidly, but a groom quickly brushed and saddled her.

Soon, Anne was aloft, and guiding her horse toward Marrenfort.

It was a mere two miles to the neighboring estate, and she pushed Angel a little to cover the distance quickly. When she reached the house, she looked up at its blank face and a momentary qualm went through her. Angel stopped and pawed at the gravel drive as Anne hesitated.

Just then the door opened and the Marquess of Marrenfort emerged, looking expectantly at Anne. "Come in, my dear. You needn't stay out here."

"Oh, Lord Marrenfort, I was just out for a ride and wondered if you'd had any news of Jamie."

He shielded his eyes and shook his head. "Nothing so far. I shouldn't worry my dear."

"One can't help it. Especially when tales of battles and attacks arrive in the newspapers Father gets."

He smiled a little condescendingly. "I wouldn't worry your pretty head over such things, Lady Anne. I'm sure you have enough to keep you busy. James will be fine. The British Navy is the best in the world, after all."

She smiled weakly and nodded. "Yes, sir. I shall leave you in peace."

"That's quite all right, my dear."

She reined her horse around and trotted off before breaking into a loping canter. Her cheeks burned in embarrassment. She had practically declared herself before him. What was he to think?

She rode past Gypsy's Gate, quelling a shudder as she did so. Her gaze was drawn inexorably toward it and after a moment, Angel turned toward the broken beam that lay like a cross-hatch on a real gate. This was formed from a tree that had fallen over from a break in the trunk, and another tree that had stopped its fall. From a distance, it looked like an overgrown and neglected gate and had been christened the Gypsy's Gate as a joke by none other than Edwin when they were children.

And there he had died.

She rode past, dragging herself and Angel away.

Daylight had waned by the time she arrived back at the stable and slid down from her horse's back. The grooms took Angel off and she made her way back up to the house that would one day be Sir Richard's.

Anne glanced at the clock as she went inside and found she was running short of time to change for supper. Once in her room she rang for her maid and began the process of divesting herself of her riding habit. Everly came in and quickly took charge of the situation. Soon she stood dressed in her periwinkle gown with silver embroidery about the bodice and a silver sash. In the mirror, her eyes sparkled with the color, and her hair looked truly ashen in the dimming light.

By the time she made it out onto the landing, the gong had rung, and she picked up her pace to make it to the dining room in time. Her father and Sir Richard were there, discussing something they had found relating to the history of Enniston. Lord Welmont nodded as soon as she arrived, and they all were seated. Anne tried not to breathe too heavily, though she was a little out of breath.

The second course was being cleared when a footman arrived carrying a salver with a letter on it. Lord Welmont frowned.

"From Marrenfort. What can they have to say?"

He set it down on the table and Anne eyed it with nervous energy.

"Please, Father, it must be of some importance if his lordship wrote so late. Perhaps there is news of Lord Ashton."

"Oh well, you may be right." He picked up the letter and broke the seal. He read and his frown deepened. "Anne, you did not mention you were at Marrenfort this afternoon."

"There has not been much call to discuss it. What does the letter say?"

"Only that an express came shortly after. Young James has been injured in a battle and is on his way home to convalesce."

Anne's fork dropped to her plate and her breath caught in her throat. She felt dizzy for a moment. Richard reached across to steady her. She took a deep breath and looked at her father.

"Does it say anything else? How badly is he hurt?"

"I daresay that is all he knows. Well, well, well. I do hope the lad makes it. Imagine how awful for his lordship to lose both sons in the space of a few months."

Anne stifled a cry and clutched her water glass, forcing it with shaking hands to her mouth. Her throat felt dry, and she could hardly speak. *Jamie wounded! Badly enough to be sent home!* She shook a little and wrapped her arms around her as she dragged in a deep breath.

"Lady Anne, are you quite well?"

"I am. Just concerned for my very old friend. I hope he is not seriously hurt." But her voice cracked on the last word and one hand went to her throat.

"What?" her father bellowed.

"Jamie. I am worried!" she all but shouted.

His brow furrowed and he cocked his ear, but she did not trust herself to speak again. Instead, she picked up her fork and concentrated on her plate. She sensed more than saw Sir Richard sit down. She stared down through the veal and tried to think past the terrible wall in her brain.

The one with words scratched upon it: *Jamie could be dead.*

Chapter Fourteen

The chill had grown into a full-fledged fever. Jamie's chest burned within him, driving him to groan and thrash as though he could escape the pain. His mind swam in delirious circles, causing him to cry out in horror at what he saw. Anne dying, Anne dead, his brother's corpse climbing from its grave... He shuddered and shook, which brought more pain.

Finally, one morning, he woke clear-headed but weak. He drank the broth offered him, and allowed Jim to shave the stubble that had taken over his jaw. Washed and dressed in clean clothes, he felt transformed. He forced himself to sit up, and leaned against the wall, right arm clamped tight against his chest as he slowly breathed in a little deeper.

"How bad do I look?"

"Well, apart from the lank hair, pasty complexion, and red eyes, Not too bad. The hollow cheeks give you a more rugged expression."

Jamie smiled weakly. "I'm not much of a sailor right now."

Jim was suddenly serious. "You survived, Jamie. That was a nasty hit. We almost lost you more than once. Others weren't so lucky. Nothing but burials at sea, it seems for days."

Jamie nodded. "What are they going to do with me?"

"I'm going to take you back to your family and make sure you survive the trip."

"Not much fear of that, surely."

"Doctor isn't quite happy with you. Wounds are only now starting to heal. The fever set you back."

"Well, I am hungry so that is a step in the right direction."

Jim left for several minutes and returned with a steaming bowl of peas and salt pork. He held it for Jamie who dished up spoon after shaking spoon into his mouth. Finally, he sat back.

"That's all I can do for now. God, it tasted good!"

Jim grinned and set the bowl aside. "It does me good to see that. You'll heal faster the more you can eat."

A wave of dizziness passed over Jamie, and he slowly lowered himself down to the pallet. Jim helped him.

"I don't know how to thank you, Jim."

"No thanks needed."

"But—"

"No, Lord Ashton. I consider you my friend, and I will do all I can to help you."

"I'm not used to that title."

"No. Changes are hard sometimes. Inheritances always come with death. Difficult to digest, somehow."

"Yes. But I can see I need to rise above it and somehow prove to my father that the lesser man did not survive."

****

The following day rose bright, sunshine sparkling on the waves. Jamie let Jim help him out onto the deck so he could sit in the light for a while. He tilted his head back, letting the sun play over his features, eyes closed against the brightness. The warmth spread over him, soaking and reviving him. He took a deeper breath, then another, braving the stabbing through his chest. His collapsed lung slowly inflated, and held. He smiled.

Soon, though, he needed to lie down once more, and Jim appeared to help him back to his pallet. A shout went up as the coast of England was spotted just as he was settling down. There was a tumult within at the thought that he was closer to seeing Anne. Only to once again feel the jab of jealousy as he wondered who she had seen that day. Who was it?

"What were you thinking just then?"

Jim startled him.

He shook his head. "Nothing, really."

"Something, really. But, you don't have to tell me."

He sighed, gritting his teeth as his chest spasmed. "Just…there's a girl…a woman that I grew up with."

"Oh?"

"I saw something that has bothered me."

"So, you love this girl."

"That is a rather bald way to put it…"

"But true. It's plain you care about her or whatever you saw would not pain you so much. What did you see?"

"She was riding, and started when she saw me, turned red and all. The way she looked, so secretive and terrified that I had seen her. Her dress was dirty and her hair disarranged. Like she had been…"

"With a man."

"Yes."

"Or come off her horse."

"Anne does not come off a horse."

"But, it happens. Could that not be it?"

Jamie's eyes opened wide at the thought. "But why so secretive?"

"That could be imagined. At any rate, give the girl a chance to explain herself."

Jamie was silent, thinking. He sighed again, and this time his chest did not tighten. "You're right, it's the least I can do. She's my oldest friend. She was also my brother's intended."

"You know this, or think this?"

"I know. They would disappear often together with no chaperone."

"How was this?"

Jamie shrugged. "Her mother is in an unconventional relationship and in no position to supervise her."

"But surely someone has been found for her?"

"I doubt her father has even thought about it. He is rather a doddering old fellow."

"Sometimes those are the best. Your girl doesn't sound like an easy sort. Perhaps there is another explanation for her relationship with your brother."

"Perhaps, but no one has questioned it. Not even her."

Another shout went up, and this time Jim rose to leave. "We're coming close to port. They'll be needing me. I'll come get you once we are moored in."

Jamie lay back and felt the bullet hole under the bandages. The stitches pulled along his spine where the bullet had been dug out and he dreaded the trip home. The only viable option was to put him in a cart, and he knew what that would feel like for a hundred or so miles. Two, three days on the road being jolted every inch of the way.

But then, Anne.

He relaxed back into the pallet, allowing himself to remember the moment he kissed her, the melding of their lips and spirits in that brief span of time. He tried to divine her feelings, but could not. Surprise, yes. Pleasure, he wasn't sure.

But she certainly had not resisted…

He sighed, enduring another stab in his chest. He could feel the ship slowing, practically see her slipping closer to their berth, the tossing of lines and the securing of the *H.M.S. Waynflete* in the Portsmouth harbor. Where would they put the *Vierge*? And, of course, the French crew.

He felt, rather than heard, the gangplank lowered and waited for what seemed like an eternity until Jim and another sailor came to help him up. He gritted his teeth and breathed shallowly as they raised him up, then let him stand a moment as his brain settled and the dizziness faded. Then, step by step he made his way out and down the gangplank with a man on either side. A cart waited at the bottom, with a pile of straw covered with blankets.

"It was the best I could do. The man will take us to your father's estate, though."

"Thank you, Jim. I don't know what I would do without you."

"Captain sent an express to your father. They will be ready for you when you arrive."

"And you must stay as my guest."

"Of course. Now, this is going to hurt…"

He and the sailor lifted Jamie up by his arms and

pulled him onto the pallet that had been prepared for him. Catching his breath as the pain shot through him, he slowly settled back into the covered hay and soon his shallow breathing deepened.

Jim's face appeared overhead, "Are you all right?"

Jamie simply nodded his head, not trusting himself to speak. Jim covered him with another blanket, then went back to get their bags which he tossed into the cart beside Jamie. Then he climbed onto the box beside the driver, and they jolted forward.

The hay helped to cushion the worst of the bumping along, but Jamie still felt every one. The sky moved overhead, framed by the roofs of buildings lining the street they were going down. It was oddly restful, despite the harsh movement of the cart up and down over cobblestones. The sound of voices and commerce going on around him faded into the background and there was only the sky and the clouds and the roofs...

He woke with a start. The day had darkened, and the cart was still. He pushed himself up to look out over the edge. They were pulled up to an inn. Jim came out and grinned upon seeing him.

"Got us a room. You'll be able to rest easy for a night."

"I seem to have slept the day away."

"I was glad to see it. The surgeon said you needed rest to heal properly."

"Where is your family, Jim?"

"Just north of London, a little town called Wexley. Father has a small estate there. No marquess, but respectable."

Jamie grunted as his feet hit the ground, jarring his

wounds. He leaned heavily upon Jim as they made their way into the inn and up the stairs, stopping frequently.

Jamie lay down on the bed and sighed. "Ahhh….I had forgotten what this felt like."

Jim laughed. "Ha, a sight better than a pile of hay I would venture. I'll be back, going to find us something to eat."

Jamie nodded, feeling truly hungry. By the time Jim came back carrying two plates, he was sitting up, ready to take one. The braised meat and vegetables tasted excellent after the ship's fare and Jamie was able to finish every scrap. Then Jim collected the dishes and carried them out. When he returned, Jamie had stripped down to his shirt and lay back upon the mattress.

Jim read a book he had picked up from a bookshelf and Jamie dozed. It was early the next morning when he was shaken lightly by Jim to waken. He sat up slowly, clutching his side, and let Jim help him dress before they went downstairs for some breakfast. Once again, Jamie savored the solid, hearty fare and then allowed the innkeeper to help Jim lift him onto his pallet in the cart. He leaned back, rested and well-fed, and girding himself for the journey.

Two days later, the cart pulled up the drive to Marrenfort. As they came over the hill, Jim let loose a whistle of appreciation and shot a glance back to where Jamie lay.

"Not bad, Lord Ashton."

Jamie chuckled. "Well, it isn't mine."

"But will be one day."

"Hmm. Yes, I can't get used to the idea. Always thought I'd work and buy myself a place with the prize money."

"A dream I share. Not quite where I need to be yet, though."

"No. But getting closer."

The door opened and Jamie sat up to see his father waiting there, pale and drawn. He looked different somehow and Jamie frowned, then gasped in pain as his feet hit the ground, jolting his chest. His father started forward, then stopped, and Jim helped Jamie into the house and up the long stairs to his room. His valet met him there and quickly undressed and washed him, placing a clean shirt over his bandages and lifting him into bed.

With a sigh of relief, Jamie leaned back against the pillows. There was a tumult in the hall and the door opened slowly to reveal Anne. She was pale, with circles under her eyes and she edged forward slowly.

"Jamie, it is really you! And you look…well."

"You can be truthful, Anne. I look awful. But better than I was."

He reached out a hand to her and she came forward to sit on the edge of the bed and take his hand in hers.

"Oh, Jamie! I have been so worried. All of us have.".

"Well, I'm home and on the mend. Just got a long way to go."

He could see no hint of a secretive nature and pushed aside the old jealousy. He was home, and she was here. That was truly all that mattered at the moment. Jim grinned behind Anne and he smiled in turn. His hand gripped Anne's more tightly and he was rewarded with the shadow of a smile from her.

Suddenly everyone pulled back as Jamie's father shuffled forward. His eyes were rimmed red and his cheeks hollow, something which confused Jamie until his father paused, then said.

"Glad to have you home, son."

"Thank you, Father. It is good to be here."

"Been worried for you."

"As you see, I am recovering."

"Thank God for that," his father burst out, then stretched a hand toward him.

After a moment, Jamie reached across to his father, and they clasped hands. The marquess nodded, disappeared, to be replaced once again by Anne and Jim.

Anne's eyes were expressive, and Jamie could not look away. But she leaned forward and let her hand fall upon his arm.

"I should go. If you like, I can come back tomorrow and read to you."

He nodded. "I should like that."

She turned to leave, and Jim said, "I'll see you to the door."

Jamie leaned back and closed his eyes, fighting the urge to call for laudanum to ease the pain in his chest. A footman entered carrying a tray and set it over his lap.

He turned his attention to his light supper and wondered where Jim had got to.

Chapter Fifteen

Anne got as far as the stairs before she stumbled. Jim caught her up and steadied her. She looked up at him and said, "Thank you. I'm sorry. It has just been such a shock."

"Yes, it has."

"And you, you have been there with him?"

"He saved my life. I couldn't leave him."

"Thank God for you, then. Will he truly be all right?"

"The ship's surgeon seemed to think so. He was able to get the bullet out, which I guess is a great thing. Jamie's heaps better than he was."

"I don't know that I could have stood to see him much worse."

"You would. I have a feeling, Lady Anne, that you would do whatever it took."

Her mouth compressed for a moment before she nodded. Stepping through the front door, the cold air hit her. She tied her scarf more securely around her neck before allowing herself to be helped onto Angel's back so she could ride home.

Her mind was a whirl. She had never imagined Jamie to look so drawn and pale. He had lost weight, as shown by the hollows of his cheeks and the indentations over his temples. The tears pressed forward at the memory, and she stifled them with a deep breath. She would not cry! He lived, and would live. Each day he would get better.

At least he seemed to have forgiven her, though she looked forward to a time when she could explain. And she would explain; she had determined on a course of honesty with the Hannigans where Elsie was concerned. They needed to know that Edwin had left a piece of himself behind.

She eyed Gypsy's Gate as she rode past. Angel seemed to sense her sudden nervousness and lifted her head. The shadows had deepened, and the trail was dark before her. They were coming into the deepest part of the wood, and an eerie sense of foreboding came over her. Not far from here Edwin had died…

Shaking herself, she gripped the reins tighter and quickened Angel's pace. They jogged down the trail, finally coming across the deepest part of the woods and out onto the other side. There, on a low hill, the lights of Enniston shone.

Angel's ears pricked forward, and she quickened her pace. Anne did not slow her, and they trotted up the hill to the stables, their breath blowing in little clouds before them. The groom rushed forward to take her by the bridle as Anne slid down and dusted off her skirt. With a final pat on her horse's shoulder, she headed back to the house.

She went straight to her room to change for supper. She was smoothing her hair as she made her way down the stairs to the dining room where her father and Sir Richard already waited. Catching her breath a little, she sat down.

"I was visiting Lord Ashton."

"Oh yes? How is he?"

"He is very weak from the journey, but his friend insists he is getting better."

"Lucky to be alive! Shots can go septic. Kill a man before you know it."

"Yes, well, his was bad, but he is recovering."

There was silence as the soup was brought in and they ate. Anne's stomach tightened, but she forced down a few spoonfuls. In her mind's eye she still saw Jamie, pale and weak, and she had to swallow against the lump in her throat. Through the courses as they came, she forced herself to eat a few bites. She sighed to herself as the pudding was brought in, grateful it was only a jelly. She took a couple of bites then set her spoon down.

Anne rose, made her way automatically to the drawing room and went to the pianoforte. Once there, she played a simple tune before going to the harp and trying to pluck out the same tune there. By the time her father and Sir Richard arrived, her fingers were sore, and she was forced to abandon the instrument.

"Keep playing, my dear!" he said loudly.

With an inaudible sigh, she returned to the pianoforte and played a couple of songs while her father sat and read. Sir Richard watched her with his hawk-like gaze and she did her best to ignore him. When she stopped playing, she glanced at her father for a moment, but he did not register that he heard anything different. She looked automatically to her mother's chair and felt a pang that it was empty. Over two years now, and she still missed her.

She went to the settee and reached for a book, only to find Sir Richard seated beside her. Startled, she found him pressing close, his hand creeping up to clasp hers.

"My dear, I must speak now. Allow me to express my utmost admiration for you, and beg you to become my wife."

Anne's gaze went first to her father, then back to Sir Richard. Her mouth moved but no sound came out and she tried to pull her hand back, only to find it truly trapped.

"I know you may have held some girlish feelings for Lord Ashton, especially given your long association. However, I think it fair to say he is unlikely to reciprocate, considering your unfortunate parentage."

Anne exerted herself and snatched back her hand, anger rising suddenly though she kept her voice down so her father would not hear. "Yes, Sir Richard, and given my unfortunate parentage, I find it surprising that you would ask for my hand."

"Not so! I have great admiration for your mother. I am not so fastidious as to expect my wife to be totally unblemished. I think my position more than outweighs any baggage yours may carry."

Anne looked at him in disbelief. "I must decline your proposition. I do not think I would make an acceptable wife for you, given my blemishes."

He faltered. "I do not say I think you blemished. You are perfection itself in my eyes."

"I cannot see how…"

"Love will cover many a fault."

"At any rate, I do not feel the same for you."

He leaned in closer. "But given time, surely your feelings would change. Think! You need never leave your home."

She pulled back from him and turned a little away.

"My answer is no, Sir Richard."

He straightened, as though finally hearing her though he distrusted his own ears. He stood and nodded goodnight to her father before squaring his shoulders and marching from the room. She sighed and leaned back against the settee, wondering how a man could propose to her under her father's very nose without his sensing it.

Anne pushed herself up from the seat and went to her father, touching him lightly on the shoulder before bending down to kiss him on the cheek. He patted her hand without looking up and she wove amongst the furniture until she reached the open hallway with its impressive staircase.

Her room was cold, though a fire burned in the grate. She changed quickly into her nightdress and her maid popped the warmer between the sheets before she got into bed. Soon, she was alone in her room with nothing but a single candle to keep her company. She pushed all thought of Sir Richard from her and curled up beneath the blankets.

Somewhere, over the next hill, Jamie lay in his own bed recovering from what could have been a mortal wound. She squeezed her eyes shut at the thought and took a deep breath to steady her nerves. He lived, and the outlook was favorable.

But what if he doesn't want me…

****

The rattle of the curtain rings woke her the next morning as her maid opened the room to let in the growing sunshine. Anne brushed her hair from her face and rubbed her eyes as she pushed up from the bed. She drew her dressing gown around her and went downstairs to the breakfast room. The room faced east, and the sunshine poured in from an unusually clear sky. Anne's spirits lifted. She would definitely ride over to Marrenfort that day.

Her plans changed when she received a note from her mother asking her to come for tea. Torn, she hesitated before answering. Slowly, she wrote indicating she would be there and went upstairs to get dressed.

Sometime later she rode out on Angel, wearing her deep blue riding habit. The pin holding her hat on pulled at her scalp with every step of the horse's hooves and she schooled herself not to wince. Normally she would not have worn a hat, but she knew her mother would want to see her well turned out.

Riding through Brumley, she nodded as she passed acquaintances. She would have gone around the village, but this was the most direct route and so she braved the gazes. She caught a few furtive looks and was certain tongues would wag about her going to visit her disgraced mother.

Evelyn Kingsley was dressed in an older gown that simply underscored to Anne her mother could not afford to get new clothes made. They hugged, and Evelyn retained her arm about Anne's waist as they went into the main room where a bright fire burned. They sat in chairs close by one another and Evelyn poured out some tea for her.

"Thank you, my dear, for coming."

"You don't often ask me."

"I hesitate to write. I know my handwriting would give your father pain."

"He rarely looks at the post, Mama. You can write

me anytime."

Evelyn smiled and took a sip of tea. She pursed her lips and looked down for a moment.

"Mama, what is wrong?"

Evelyn sighed and set her cup down. "I think it best to say it outright before you hear it from someone else. A story has got round that Edwin's ghost is haunting that place where he died. A few people claim to have seen it and the whole village talks of little else. I am worried for I know Lord Ashton has just returned. What if he hears of this?"

"Oh, Mama, I don't think it will distress him. He will be angry, I'm sure, but not distressed."

"I am glad of that, but still. It is senseless talk that can only cause harm, yet I don't know what to do to stop it."

Anne blew out a breath and shook her head. "There is nothing we can do, I suppose. Now poor Edwin will go down in local legend as the ghost of Gypsy's Gate." She made a moue of distaste and picked up her cup.

They sat in silence for a time. Evelyn cut a slice of cake for Anne and they ate.

Finally, Anne said, "Is that everything you wished to tell me…?"

Evelyn replaced her cup in its saucer. "Not entirely, no. How is Lord Ashton?"

"He is recovering, which is the best news. He very nearly died, though he would deny that. The gentleman who brought him home indicated as much."

"What gentleman is this?"

"Do you know, I don't remember being introduced. It was all such a jumble. I do remember Jamie calling him Jim, though."

"And is he handsome?"

Anne frowned. "Yes, quite. Why would that matter?"

"No reason. But I am so glad Lord Ashton had someone to look after him on the journey home."

"Yes. I suppose I will learn more when next I visit."

"When will that be?"

Anne sighed. "I don't know. Tomorrow I guess, unless I am needed at home. I should probably work in the herb garden before winter frosts everything."

"Are you keeping it up?"

"As much as I am able. Helen—you remember the housekeeper—does quite a lot."

"Yes, she always liked being in the garden."

They were silent for a time, then Anne set her plate down and rose. "Mama, I should get back. I will find a way to tell Jamie about the local gossip so he won't be taken unawares." She hugged her mother and held her tightly for a moment before releasing her. "It is so silly, though."

"I know, and I dislike the implication that he has unfinished business. If only they would let him lie in peace."

Anne went out and untied her horse, then climbed into the saddle and arranged her skirt. She looked down at her mother who smiled up at her. "Goodbye, Mama!"

"Goodbye, my dear."

Anne guided Angel away and this time they climbed up the rise to ride behind the village in an arc toward the road to Enniston. They cantered for a ways, then Anne pushed her to a gallop before pulling up onto the road and jogging steadily for a time. Angel was full of spirit, and her step continually quickened without prompt. Anne was forced to hold her head back to keep her from taking the bit and breaking into a run.

By the time they reached Enniston, Angel had calmed and was walking staidly along. Almost she continued on to Marrenfort, but it was getting late, and Angel had been out much of the day already. Instead of going into the house, she reined her toward the woods between the two estates. As she thought about what she had learned, her step increased in speed until she stood on the rise overlooking the break in the woods where Gypsy's Gate stood.

The afternoon shadows were merging into twilight as she stared down at the broken tree. From her vantage, it looked very little like an actual gate, but Edwin had always been imaginative. She was about to turn when she caught movement.

Anne focused, staring at the spot where something had been just a moment before. A squirrel chattered in a nearby tree and crickets sang, but otherwise it was quiet. Had she seen something, or not? She shook her head and turned away, nevertheless feeling spooked. Her step was quicker than it might normally have been as she headed back toward Enniston.

Night had fallen by the time she reached her home. She changed quickly and was late going in to supper. Her father had begun without her and looked up in disapproval when she came in.

"Where were you?"

"I'm so sorry, Father."

"Yes, yes, but where were you?"

She sighed. "I was out riding. I stopped by to see Mother."

"Ah."

He stared at her for a moment before picking up his fork and knife and cutting a piece of the beefsteak. He ate in silence for some time, and Anne quickly finished her soup to catch up with him. Her steak was tough, and she gave up on trying to eat it after just a couple of bites.

"And how is…er…your mother?"

Anne stared. It was the first mention of Evelyn Kingsley in almost two years. "She is well, Father. Thank you for asking."

He cleared his throat. "Good, good. Have you any news of Lord Ashton?"

"No, I was unable to visit him today. I am planning on going over tomorrow."

"Good, good." He cleared his throat again. "Sir Richard has gone off."

"What? I thought he was staying through to Friday."

"He suddenly remembered an engagement and rushed off. Strange, I would not have thought him forgetful."

"Ah well, he knows his own business best."

She pushed all thought of Sir Richard aside. Anne's head was a whirl with the story told by her mother. She did not believe in ghosts. Did she? What had she seen? Nothing, she was certain. But what had others seen?

She set her spoon down and said, "May I be excused, Father?"

"Of course, of course. Off you go…"

She rose, went to her room and sat on the chaise beside the window. Pushing the curtain aside she peered out onto the lawn, trying to think again of what she had seen.

She shut the curtain and sat back, drawing the lap blanket over her and thinking.

Chapter Sixteen

Jamie sat in the sunshine, the invalid chair positioned so that the sun did not hit his eyes. He leaned back, pulling the blanket closer as the air was unseasonably cold. He had insisted on going out, and Jim had dutifully pushed him out into the fresh air.

He still marveled at how still it was on land. The ground did not move beneath one's feet, but was solid and quiet. Then he remembered silent nights on board the ship, sails full and the ship running fast through the water with barely a sound. Two kinds of stillness, and he did not know which he preferred.

He shifted in his seat, trying not to look down the drive and watch for Anne. He had expected her all the day before. And she had not come.

She hadn't come.

What was he to make of that? His situation, though not so dire as it had been, was still precarious. He thought that if she cared, she would have come to see him. Had something prevented her? Or had she simply not been inclined to inquire as to his wellbeing?

He blew out a breath and looked around for Jim. He'd expressed a desire to go off walking and had not yet returned. He heard distant hoofs and glanced up quickly. He recognized Angel and Anne…and Jim.

Something twisted inside him at the sight. Jim stepped closer to Angel and helped Anne down. She thanked him nicely—too nicely?—and stepped toward him.

"Oh, this does my heart good to see you out here! The fresh air has revived you!"

Her eyes were alight as she looked at him and he could not stay angry for long.

"Thanks again to Jim."

"You must excuse me, Jim, but we haven't been properly introduced."

Jim's mouth fell open in a bark of laughter and Jamie buried his face in his palm. "All the excitement... Lady Anne Debenham, may I introduce Mr. James Knight."

Anne curtseyed with a smile and Jim bowed.

"There, now we may talk."

But she smiled as she said it and again something sharp twisted in his breast.

"What have you been doing?" he said rather abruptly.

Anne looked at him with surprise, but answered evenly, "My mother asked me to go see her. She asked me to relay some rather disagreeable news."

Jamie frowned. "What is it?"

"The villagers are saying that Gypsy Gate is being haunted by your brother. Apparently several people are claiming to have seen his ghost."

"What!"

"I know. It is ridiculous."

"It's monstrous!"

"But Jamie, I thought I saw something, too."

He sat mute. Jim cleared his throat. "Can you tell us what you think you saw?"

"That's just it, I don't know. I thought I saw

something move, but when I looked, nothing was there."

"So you think—"

"No! But there may be a trick of the light there that has misled some people."

"What do you suggest?"

"We should probably look into it. When you are up to it, that is."

"Why not walk down now?" suggested Jamie, regretting it the instant after.

Anne's eyebrows flew up and she looked at Jim. "If you would feel better about it, certainly I can go look now." She tied Angel to a tree.

"I'll accompany you," said Jim.

Jealousy warred with reason inside, and Jamie forced himself to breathe deeply to remain calm. The two figures disappeared over the crest of the hill, and he struggled to stand so he could see them. His legs were weak, and a slight dip to one side caused him to overcorrect and lose balance. He tumbled in a heap, agonizing pain shooting through his chest.

It took several long moments before the sensations stabilized and he took in his situation. He lay in an inglorious jumble beside the invalid chair. Slowly he untangled his legs and pushed himself back up to a crawling position. The indignity of it all turned quickly to anger and he pulled himself back into the chair, falling back with a sharp breath out. His chest hurt, his knees were stained, and he felt utterly humiliated.

Looking out toward Gypsy's Gate, Jamie saw the two figures moving slowly about. He could not tell what they were doing, only that they were there, together. The rage had died by now. There stood two of the dearest people in the world to him, and he would not stand in their way.

When Anne and Jim returned, Jamie was quiet. Anne sat down next to Jamie's chair and breathed out a long sigh.

"Oh Lord, it's farther than it looks."

"It is," Jim said. "But there's nothing suspicious there at all."

"No, I couldn't see anything strange that might explain what people have seen."

"Well, good thing you two went and checked," Jamie said.

"Anything, if it eases your mind," Jim said.

"Can you take me back?"

"Of course." Jim jumped up and took hold of the chair, turned it around and pushed it back toward the house.

Anne touched the stain on his knee. "What have you been up to?"

Jamie batted her hand away. "I just fell out of the chair. No harm done." It came out harsher than he intended, and his cheeks went hot with embarrassment.

Anne's eyes widened at his tone, but she left the subject alone. They made their way in relative silence back to the manor. When they reached the front of the house, Anne made to climb up onto Angel's saddle, and Jim went instantly to her side to help her up. She settled herself and her skirt and then looked at Jamie with a slight frown.

"I am glad to see you so well recovered, Lord Ashton."

He nodded without really looking at her. His spirit fell with each hoofbeat that carried her further away. He looked up to see Jim's face, his frown mirroring Anne's.

"What happened?"

"I don't know what you mean?"

"You were fine, then changed all of a sudden."

Jamie struggled for something to say. "I was embarrassed. Falling. You know."

"But you should know neither of us would have cared except that you might be hurt."

Jamie could only look away, anxious to hide his true feelings. Jim helped him up the stairs and then into the front sitting room. After settling him into a chair nearest the fire, he rang for some refreshment to be brought.

Soon enough there were sandwiches and tea, and Jim frowned anew to see how little Jamie ate. Jamie stared at the fire, afraid to look at his friend.

"Jamie?"

"Hmm?"

"What's wrong? Truly, you do not look well all of a sudden."

Jamie shrugged and sighed, leaning back. "It is just very depressing being such an invalid. I wanted to be exploring the gate with you. Instead, I fell. Embarrassing."

He glanced up to see if Jim would accept the explanation. He seemed to, for his lips pursed and he nodded.

"I can see that. But you must know that there is nothing to be embarrassed of, especially in front of Lady Anne and myself."

The fact that Jim used her title somehow lifted his spirits; it implied a distance between them. He tried to smile and reached for another sandwich. There passed a little silence.

Then Jim said, "She cares about you, Jamie. Deeply."

Heartened, Jamie noted his tense expression. "Is there someone you think about?"

"There could be. I don't know, however. There are many obstacles in the way."

Jamie frowned, wondering if he was referring to Anne and the day felt overcast once more.

Jim seemed to shake himself and leaned back. "Have you exhausted yourself, yet?"

"Very nearly. I am getting stronger, though."

"You aren't coughing up blood anymore, and you are able to stay on your feet for longer. I'd say that's improvement!"

"Well, help me upstairs so I can rest. I am impatient to be up and about."

"That was a nasty shot you took. Best take it slow."

Jamie walked, with support, back to his room where he leaned back upon his pillows with a sigh. "How long are you going to stay, Jim?"

"As long as you need me, though I suppose any one of these servants would do as well."

"Not for the company, though. Does me good to have you about."

But he thought about Anne, and questioned this. Part of him wanted Jim far away. He pushed such feelings aside, however and looked with gratitude at his friend.

"I shall have to return to the ship, soon. I suppose I shall just have to be ready when the order comes." He picked up a book, opened it to the place he had left off, and began to read.

Jamie gazed out the window and wished Anne had stayed longer. He wanted, no, needed, time alone with her to discern her true feelings. Was she still in love with Edwin? Did she have someone else? Where had she been that day he caught her coming home with a dirty skirt and mussed hair?

He must have slept, for when next he opened his eyes, his valet was there, pulling clothing out at Jim's instruction.

"What is happening?"

"We're getting you dressed for supper. I think you are strong enough to make it."

"I don't know, after today I may be done in."

But he let them dress him in his dark blue jacket and tie his cravat in one of the newest styles. Jim disappeared to his room and arrived similarly dressed and they headed off for the stairs.

He managed to make it all the way to the dining room, relying only slightly on Jim. When he stepped in, his father looked up in surprise and then turned away, blinking rapidly.

Gruffly, he said, "Good to see you. And you, Mr. Knight, are welcome at my table."

They sat and the first course was brought out. Jim followed Jamie's example and the two grinned at that.

His father cleared his throat. "I saw you outside today. Was that wise?"

"Dr. Hamilton assured me it would be good if I felt up to it. I perhaps stayed out a little too long, but overall I feel much improved."

"Good, good. I am glad to hear it. And you, Mr. Knight, have you everything you need?"

"Indeed, yes, sir. Your staff has been very helpful."

"Excellent. As they should be." He lapsed into a silence then as he concentrated upon eating.

Jamie ate the venison stew with real appreciation. A footman brought in a letter which he handed to Jim. who took one look at it and shot a glance at Jamie.

"From Captain Ellis. I think I may be leaving." He read over the short note and nodded. "Being called back, with hopes that you are doing well."

A hole opened up within Jamie.

His father said only, "We've been glad to have you. I shall send my thanks to your captain for allowing you time to stay and get James situated."

Jim folded the letter and set it aside. A silence fell over the small company as they worked their way through the courses. Jamie found he wasn't as hungry as he had been and set his fork down.

He was at a crossroads, he knew. Recover and return to the navy, or give up his commission and come home to stay. It was difficult. He had relished his career built on his own work, and not on his name. But his father looked withered tonight, a mere shade of himself in a huge mansion. He sighed and leaned back against the chair.

"Are you tired?" Jim asked.

Jamie shook his head. "No, just thinking."

"Well, spit it out. What are you thinking?" his father said, a trifle testily.

"What to do. Stay in the navy, or give up my commission."

His father looked up. "I should think that has an easy answer. You give up your commission and come home. Twice now you have barely escaped death. No

155

more, James."

"But I have been working at this since I was—"

"Too long. Too much. I'm not giving any more of my sons. You'll stay home. Mr. Knight, do forgive our manners."

"Not at all," Jim said.

The room fairly echoed with silence after his father's outburst. Jamie stared at the pudding placed before him. He lifted a spoon and took a bite, then another. His mind seethed with thoughts and partial plans to return to the navy. It was a matter of pride, he knew, but that didn't change anything. He wanted to go back to being a lieutenant with aspirations of becoming a captain of his own vessel one day.

He set down his spoon and his napkin, then rose with a stiff nod to his father. Jim immediately jumped up, but Jamie forestalled him. "Finish your meal. I'll get the footman to help me up the stairs."

Jim slowly sat down, and Jamie made his way to the hall where he flagged down a servant to support him up the stairs and to his room. Once there, his valet undressed him and helped him into bed. It felt good to slip between the sheets and rest after the trying day. His mind, though, would not settle.

There were two things he needed to accomplish: return to the navy, and marry Anne.

Chapter Seventeen

Anne had explored Gypsy's Gate thoroughly, but found no sign of anything that could be construed as a ghost. Mr. Knight had been gentlemanly, and she approved of his obvious care and concern for Jamie. Somehow, it always came back to Jamie.

She rode Angel back to the stable where a groom came forward to take her. Anne waved them away and proceeded to remove the saddle and brush her out. The long strokes with the brush helped calm both the horse and her. By the time she was done grooming Angel, she felt better.

After releasing her horse into her stall and topping up the hay with some grain, she patted her one last time. The house seemed to loom over her as she neared it, but she pushed the fanciful thought away and went inside.

She found the servants rushing about in a near frenzy and stopped the housekeeper, who shooed off a maid,

"Yes, Lady Anne?"

"What is going on? Has something happened?"

"Lady Targetty is coming for a visit. She just announced it in a letter to your father. We are working to get ready."

Anne's heart sank. "Oh, I see. Thank you."

She sighed to herself and made her way up the

stairs to the drawing room. A maid knelt, polishing the brass knobs of the grate. She thought about going to the piano, but just then the maid rose and made her way to the candelabra sitting on the pianoforte. Anne went upstairs.

The doors to the Empire Room were open at the end of the hall. She was sure the windows were open to air it and fresh linens were being laid on the bed. She looked for her father and found him in his room.

"Papa!" she shouted.

He looked up, his mustache sticking out somewhat. "Yes, my dear?"

"I just heard Aunt Gertrude is coming. When will she be here?"

"Tomorrow!"

"Tomorrow? Why such short notice?"

He tossed the letter he held onto the desk. "She had gone to Gloucester and dislikes it there. We are a convenient stop on her way home."

"I see. Rather hard on the servants."

He grunted, and she wondered if he had heard her completely. She raised her voice and said, "Are you still playing backgammon?"

"No! I have put off my friends so that I can oversee things here."

"I can do that, Papa! You go visit your friends."

"It's already done, wrote Hershey and Pault myself just now."

She went out into the hall and removed the letters which she found waiting to be picked up. Carrying them back to her father, she handed them to him and kissed his cheek. "Go play backgammon. I can handle getting things ready for Aunt Gertrude."

His forehead creased as he looked at her, "If you are sure…"

"Of course. I will speak to the cook and Mrs. Stevens. Go get ready." His mustache tipped up at the ends and he nodded before heading off.

She watched him go fondly, then went in search of the cook.

****

Hours later, she sat alone in the dining room, eating her supper. Her father was dining out at his friend's, and she had requested a light supper only. She carefully cut the meat from the quail and placed it in her mouth as she wondered what Jamie was doing, and what she was going to do with her indomitable aunt for a week.

Lady Targetty was her mother's aunt, but had disowned her when she went off with Havers. Instead, she had cleaved to Anne and her father, as though attention to them would make up for the loss of Evelyn. She was wont to announce her coming quickly and stay for prolonged periods. Anne suspected it was to save on housekeeping costs.

She rose and went to the sitting room. The fire burned in the fireplace, and she sat beside it, staring into the flames, thinking about Jamie. In a way she was grateful to her aunt for coming as it would distract her from constantly thinking and wondering about him.

The next morning her father met her in the breakfast room, smiling and patting her on the cheek.

"Thank you, my dear. It was a very pleasant evening. Everything seems to be in order for your aunt."

"Yes, Papa. All is ready. I spoke to Mrs. Jones about meals, and she remembered that Aunt Gertrude does not like asparagus and prefers two-minute eggs for breakfast."

"Well, that seems all right. Thank you."

She wondered if she had time to ride over to Marrenfort. Her aunt was due in the afternoon sometime, and given the distance, she thought it would be later rather than sooner. She ran upstairs to change and then went to the stable to collect Angel.

The day was pale gray, with high, overcast clouds blocking the sun for the most part. Angel was wont to kick up her heels, so Anne let her run for half a mile or so, then pulled her up as they went through the woods. When they passed Gypsy's Gate, she tried not to stare, but could not help it. Nothing moved, except a bird that landed on a branch.

"And that is all that happened that day, probably." She kicked Angel into a canter, and they rose up the hill to the house.

She was announced and waited in the drawing room. Mr. Knight and Jamie were there, and both looked up, eyes wide and eyebrows high in their foreheads.

"Jamie, Mr. Knight! I just thought I'd ride over and check on you."

Jamie's cheeks had more color, and he looked rested. "I am well, but Jim here is about to leave us."

She frowned, "I am sorry to hear that, Mr. Knight. I know Jamie will be lost without you."

The carriage was announced, and Jim bent over her hand very nicely. She smiled as she waved to him. When the carriage had pulled off, she turned to Jamie.

"How are you doing? You are up!"

"Yes, for a few minutes at a time. Still need the

invalid chair if I am going far."

"Well, are you up for a visit? I mainly came by to check on you."

"No, I'd like you to stay." He gazed down at her.

"Of course." She let him lead her into the drawing room where he seated her and then sat in a nearby chair.

"What have you been doing with yourself?.."

"Mmm. Getting ready for Aunt Gertrude."

He recoiled and made a face. "Ah. When is the happy event?"

"Today. This afternoon, sometime. Certainly in time for supper if I know Aunt Gertrude."

"So...what are your plans?"

She sighed and compressed her lips. "I have no plans. Just here to see you."

He smiled and reached a hand to her. After a moment, she slipped her own into it. He looked at their hands for a moment, then up at her. They stared into each other's eyes as the clocked ticked on..

"James?"

His father's voice echoed in the room and Anne snatched her hand back. Jamie turned to him.

"Yes, Father?"

"Ah, you have company. Hello, Lady Anne."

"Lord Marrenfort. I hope I am not intruding."

"Of course not. I was going to make the rounds and wondered if James wished to go as well. If so, I would call the carriage."

"Oh, of course," said Jamie, with a glance at Anne.

"Excellent. I shall call you when it is here, it should have delivered young Mr. Knight by now. You may finish your visit." He stepped off and Jamie turned back to Anne.

"I'm sorry. I felt I should go."

"As you should. You're the heir now. Lots to catch up on."

She rose and he followed, a little stilted, and she reached suddenly to help him. Her hands fell upon his chest, and he straightened, looking deep into her eyes. One hand cupped the back of her neck and he bent to kiss her.

She melted against him, her mouth molding against his as he pressed downward, his lips taking hers in a way that caused her heart to beat wildly in her chest. Her hands went up to his shoulders as his arm pulled her closer. She broke away to breathe, and said in a throaty voice,

"Jamie…"

"Anne. I need to know…Are you still grieving for Edwin?"

"We were not engaged."

"Yes but that would not stop you grieving."

"I did not love him, if that is what you wish to know."

He frowned. "And yet you went out with him unchaperoned."

She pushed away and stepped back. "I know what it looked like, but you must understand—"

"James, the carriage is here."

Anne turned away and reached down to straighten her skirt. She did not look at Jamie as she went out the door to where Angel stood waiting.

"Anne!." Jamie called.

Anne lifted her gaze to his, then climbed into the saddle, and rode off without a word to him. She urged Angel into a canter. The wind rushed against her face.

They careened down the hill, and then towards the woods.

Gypsy's Gate stood off to one side, and this time she saw it.

A figure had appeared beside the gate.

She pulled Angel up and stared. She struggled for a breath, only to frown and breathe out in sudden anger. There was no ghost there, just a man poking about. One of the villagers, no doubt. Simple curiosity.

She urged Angel onward, a little more forcefully than necessary and the horse burst forward, nearly unseating her. She maintained her seat in the saddle and apologized to Angel with a gentle pat on her shoulder. They cantered off toward Enniston. Anne's sudden anger turned to tears as she fought to keep them at bay.

The groom took Angel. Anne pulled out a handkerchief to wipe her eyes and headed up to the house. She went straight to her room, only to hear her name called out from the landing,

"Anne!"

Aunt Gertrude stood there, white hair piled artistically over her straight, slender form. She wore old-fashioned clothes—a long waisted jacket over a wide skirt—exquisitely made. Anne scrunched the handkerchief up in her hand to hide it. It would not do to show weakness before Aunt Gertrude.

"Yes, ma'am. I was not expecting you so soon."

"Out taking exercise, I see."

"Er, yes. I went to visit Ja—Lord Ashton. He was wounded, you know."

"No, I did not. He is recovering well, I take it?"

"Yes, indeed. Quite well."

"Excellent. He is needed at home now that his

brother is dead. Speaking of which, why aren't you in mourning?"

"I…we were not engaged."

"Ah. You are a cold-hearted thing."

"No, ma'am," Anne protested.

"Switched to the new lord, now, have you?"

"No! We are friends."

"Friends to lovers, common story."

Anne's mouth dropped open, but she shut it. Aunt Gertrude would always have the final word and it was best to simply stop.

"Is your room comfortable, Aunt?"

"Indeed, yes. Pity the room faces west, but that can't be helped I suppose."

"Do you need anything?"

"My maid is seeing to all that. I hope your staff are helpful. Pickett will certainly let me know."

"Yes, ma'am."

"Well, come on then, show me how well you play now."

"It is just about as it was…"

"Oh, surely not! You must have practiced."

Anne went to the pianoforte and sat down before taking a deep breath and sorting through the music. She started and played it through with only one or two misfingerings. When she had finished, she waited.

"Not bad. Not good enough to catch Lord Ashton, I'll wager. Certainly not with a mother who's run off in a most disgraceful way. Lord Peregrine, now, you might tempt him. Pity you aren't doing the Season this year. I'm sure we could find someone for you."

Anne pursed her lips and twined her fingers in her lap.

Her aunt rapped out a new command. "Well, come now. Let's hear you on the harp."

Anne slowly stood and walked to the harp as though to a guillotine. It had been her aunt's dearest wish that she learn the instrument, and she had never really taken to it. She swallowed, then began. By the time she finished, her aunt's eyes were closed, and her mouth was a grim line.

"You are not practicing. What did we get you that music master for if you aren't going to practice what he taught you?"

"I'm sorry, Aunt."

"Sorry? I should say you are sorry. What have you been doing with your time if not practicing your music?"

"I do ride quite frequently."

"Ride? And yet that does not entertain guests in an evening. I have hardly been on a horse in my life and yet look at me! Married well above my station, purely on the merits of my musical ability. You have a titled father, yes, but you have the shame your mother introduced to overcome."

Anne sat silent, anger rising in her even as she fought to keep it down. Just then her father ambled along and caught sight of them. He made to escape, but Aunt Gertrude had spied him.

"Lord Welmont! Ah! How lovely to see you. I was looking over my niece. Her musical ability leaves much to be desired. How are the roses?"

"Eh, what?"

"Music. Roses."

Anne rose. "I must go check on supper."

As she left she heard the two of them battling to be

heard and understood. She shot quickly downstairs to find the kitchen in an uproar. One of the kitchen maids had been badly burned and was being tended to by Mrs. Stevens. The cook waved Anne off, saying all would be ready on time, so she checked on the maid before going back upstairs.

Her father must have taken Aunt Gertrude out to personally inspect the roses, for the hall and drawing room were silent. Anne finally made her way to her room so that she could change into more acceptable attire. Her maid helped her dress, and then fixed her hair. Although it was a bit early to dress for supper, she sat in her chaise by the window and looked out, grateful to have a moment to think finally.

Jamie had kissed her yet again! And she leaned back and let the deliciousness of that moment well up within her. Her body had wakened in ways she had never dreamed of, and the fire ignited still burned despite their argument and even Aunt Gertrude. She loved him, as she always had, but now it hurt to be away from him.

Why every time they came close together, they ended up fighting? What was there in them that caused such conflict?

Somehow, they needed to get beyond it and find some way to understand one another!

Chapter Eighteen

Jamie sat in the carriage, watching the scenery go by. His father seemed withdrawn, and he wondered why. Perhaps it was because Edwin was not sitting in his spot. He put the thought aside. Everyone, Anne included, needed to get used the fact that Edwin was gone.

Anne. He closed his eyes, wondering again why they fought every time they kissed. What did it mean? Would they never be able to connect peacefully and completely? He mentally shook himself and looked up to find his father's gaze upon him.

"Are you up to this?"

"Yes, I think so. I remember wanting to go with you when I was younger."

"We are stopping first at the Platt farm. Their daughter just married the son of a Brumley innkeeper. Their son is fourteen and helps on the farm. Mrs. Platt was recently quite ill and they have incurred some medical bills as a result."

Jamie nodded as the carriage stopped. The family assembled by the front door. They were welcomed into the farmhouse and settled closest to the fire in what he was certain were the farm couple's chairs.

They sat on a rather worn settee while his father spoke quietly with them.

"Mr. Platt, how do you do?"

"Well, sir. Me and my family is well."

"How is the farm going?"

"Hay is growing good. Oats is still too early. Kitchen garden is doing well."

"As is ours. Tell me, do you put your food scraps out in it to enrich the soil?"

"Missus insists. I say it draws vermin."

"It may do, but I understand it draws our chickens, which keep the bugs down."

"Tha's a thought."

"Mrs. Platt, how are you doing?" Jamie asked when a little silence fell.

"Well, sir, thank 'ee. Doctor saw me through."

"Yes, I have instructed him to send the rest of the bills to me," Lord Marrenfort said.

The couple looked at one another, then Mr. Platt said, "Thank 'ee, sir, but—"

"Nonsense. I sent Dr. Smythe and so I must bear the cost."

He chatted quite comfortably about crops and sheep for a few more minutes and then they rose to leave. They shook hands and soon were on their way to the next farm.

His father, though not a warm man, had been kind and interested in his tenants. He'd even remembered to ask about the married daughter and questioned the son.

"How do you remember everything?"

"Practice. And true interest. I do care about them; I take my responsibilities seriously."

"What does Jeffers, the steward, do?"

"He handles the business end of things. Crops and tithes and how much hay we need for the winter, that sort of thing."

"I see. I have a lot to learn."

"Yes. And not much time, I'm afraid."

"What do you mean?" Jamie frowned, suddenly very focused on his father.

The marquess cleared his throat, looking off over the grounds through the window. His father grew quite red, and seemed to struggle with words for a moment.

"Mrs. Platt isn't the only one to have needed Dr. Smythe's expertise. The ague I can't seem to get over is a disease of the lungs, it seems. He thinks it will worsen over the course of a year or two, not much longer I'm afraid."

Jamie's breath exploded from him. His mouth opened as he fought to speak as a landed fish fights to breathe, but no sound came out. A minute passed.

"I'm sorry, James. I know this is more than you had bargained for."

"Yes, Father. Is there nothing that can be done?"

"It's true, I have yet to visit a doctor in Harley Street, but Smythe feels certain of his diagnosis."

"We must get you to Harley Street. There must be something that can be done."

His father's eyes warmed, and he smiled shortly. "Yes, son. We will."

They rode in heavy silence the rest of the tour and Jamie found it all overwhelming in light of his father's pronouncement. Still he focused on each tenant, saw how his father addressed concerns, divined needs. There was a side here he had never known, and would now know for so short a time.

They arrived back at the manor house in time to change for supper. Jamie was exhausted from the demands of the day and lay back on his bed for a moment. His valet peered in on him.

"Sir, are you dressing tonight?"

"Yes, Hinton. Just a moment." He stared up at the ceiling and felt his future close in around him. Now, certainly, he must give up his career and take on his brother's mantle.

His father was dying.

Jamie's throat constricted and he took a deep breath to gain control. Even now his father would be on his way downstairs to the dining room to fulfill his expected duties. He, Jamie, had no excuse not to do the same.

Dressing as quickly as he could, he made his way slowly down the stairs with his valet's help and into the dining room. He sat rather heavily in his accustomed spot, but his father waved him to Edwin's chair.

"Time to fulfill your duties."

Jamie moved to the seat his father indicated and that simple act seemed to bring everything crashing down upon him. His hand shook a little as he picked up the spoon, but he controlled it quickly and managed to make it through the meal. When they had finished, his father poured him a glass of port and they sat silently in the room drinking his father's excellent year.

Jamie lay in bed that night, unable to stop his brain from running in circles. How quickly life had turned on him. From unappreciated second son to heir in the course of a few months. And his father—it was as though they were finally seeing each other and now it must be cut short.

Unless there was a miracle waiting in Harley Street.

He would hold onto that hope, that there was a

mistake or that something could be done to lift the death sentence his father now lived under. Finally, his mind shifted to Anne, and he felt a settling within himself. A troubled sleep eased over him.

Morning came late to him. He was still in bed when Dr. Smythe arrived to investigate his wounds. The doctor listened to his chest and declared his progress good. The wounds were closed and healing well.

As the doctor was putting his instruments away, Jamie asked, "Is there really no hope for my father?"

Smythe's hands paused in their work. He cleared his throat and said, "In my opinion, no. I have encouraged him to seek other counsel in this matter, however. Someone with more expertise in this area."

Jamie nodded. "I just don't want to accept the possibility of losing him now."

The doctor's lips compressed in sympathy. "I will check on you again."

"Can I ride?"

"As long as you take it easy, No mad gallops or jumps over fences or anything."

"No, of course not. Thank you, Doctor."

He sat for a few minutes, shifting under the bandages a little and thinking about his day. He wanted to ride over to Enniston, then remembered that the indomitable Aunt Gertrude would be there. Did he really want to face that sharp old woman?

No, but he did want to see Anne.

He sighed and pushed himself up from the bed. His valet arrived in time to help him dress, though he needed increasingly less in that department. Once he was dressed with his boots pulled on, he headed downstairs for some breakfast and then to the stables where Phaeton stood in his stall.

He went in with the halter and easily slipped it onto his head so that he could lead him out and brush him down. By then a groom had arrived and helped as they brushed the horse and saddled him, finally putting the bridle on and handing Jamie the reins. He required help getting onto the saddle, his chest still raw and unable to take the strain of climbing up. He grinned as he urged Phaeton forward and felt the response beneath him.

After so long without much exercise, Phaeton fairly danced forward and Jamie subdued the desire to let him run. Instead, he let the horse break into a loping canter and set off down the drive toward Enniston.

The sun shone overhead, obscured only now and then by silver-white clouds. The light on his shoulders warmed him, and the heady freedom helped mask the dark thoughts that had plagued him.

He tried not to look at Gypsy's Gate as he passed, but could not help but stare intently for any sign of something supernatural. Nothing except the sunshine on the slope of the fallen tree and a bird taking off from one of the branches. He turned to focus on the road ahead.

Enniston appeared as he climbed the slight rise and came out of the woods. He rode forward and pulled up before the house, only to hear voices. He followed the sound until he came around to the rose gardens in the back. There, Anne and her aunt stood before a very old rose bush.

"I must take a cutting from this. It is exquisite."

"I will certainly ask Father. He is very proud of this bush. Jamie! How pleasant! And on Phaeton…"

"Yes, I wondered if you would ride with me."

"Oh, yes, Anne. Do ride with Lord Ashton. I am of no importance."

"Nonsense, Aunt. I cannot leave my company. I'm sure you understand. But, please join us!" she added looking up at him.

"If you are certain I won't be in the way…"

"Not at all. Here, let me hold him while you get down. Do you need help?"

"No, I think I can manage…there. Down on my own."

She quickly waved over a servant to take the horse to the stable and the three of them headed back to the house.

"How are you healing from your injuries?"

"Quite well, Lady Targetty. I thank you."

"And your father, is he well?"

A pause. "Well enough."

But Anne looked at him with a slight frown and he simply stared down at the ground. It was not the time or place to say more.

Lady Targetty chattered on about roses as they went, requiring only the occasional acknowledgement from the two of them. Jamie caught Anne's eye and smiled, to be rewarded by a secretive smile back.

His heart soared, and he nearly reached out to take her hand, stopping himself just in time. If only the aunt were gone, he could talk to her and explain himself. But as he looked over at her again, and caught her looking back at him, he knew he need not explain anything.

She understood him. She always did.

Chapter Nineteen

Anne walked beside Jamie, feeling the sunshine on her soul for the first time in days. He had smiled at her, and she thought she could fly. But, a cloud came over her mood suddenly, for there was something wrong.

"And then, of course, he courted me for several months as you would expect. His father was part of the Privy Council for the younger King George, and the stories he would tell. I still don't believe what he said about Queen Charlotte, but there, I won't gossip about our queen."

Anne nodded and asked the expected question, though she had heard this story often enough and knew the answer. "And when did he declare himself?"

"Ah! At the Chartrelles' ball. We were dancing, and I twisted my ankle coming around a very difficult step. He helped me to a chair and sent the servants running for ice. Then, as, he chafed my ankle having ascertained my permission, I said, 'I don't know what I would have done without you.' And he said, 'You need never be without me. Allow me to declare myself and beg for your hand in marriage.'"

"Quite romantic," said Jamie.

Anne shot him a look, but he seemed perfectly innocent.

"Indeed, it was. And of course Maria Spellworth accused me of pretending to sprain my ankle in order to secure him, which was utter nonsense of course. How could I have known he was about to propose?"

"How indeed. And then you were married."

"On the seventh of October, 1756. His father set us up in a little country house, and then, of course, we moved to the estate after his father's death."

"And were you happy?"

"Happy? I suppose so, though that is a very modern idea. We were well-suited, and luckily I was not given to histrionics when certain unavoidable issues arose."

"No children?" asked Jamie.

"One, but we lost her as an infant. I poured myself into charitable duties. And, of course, my sister's children and their issue."

By this time, they had reached the house and made their way to the morning sitting room where Anne rang for tea after settling her aunt. She managed to seat herself beside Jamie and they shared a secretive glance. Jamie's knee brushed Anne's and she smiled up at him.

Tea was brought in, and Anne moved to pour out, serving her aunt first.

Aunt Gertrude sipped the tea and sighed. "Ah! Noble beverage."

"I like coffee," Jamie said and earned a sharp tap from the back of Anne's hand.

Luckily, Aunt Gertrude was busy nibbling on a fresh biscuit.

"Your cook does these quite well. A little thick, perhaps, but really quite well."

"I shall tell her you said so."

"Never compliment servants, my dear. It gives them airs."

Jamie looked at Anne and flashed his eyebrows. She bent her head to hide her smile and to choke down the giggle that had threatened.

Aunt Gertrude set her cup down and fixed Jamie with a boiled gooseberry stare. "Now, Lord Ashton, what are your plans now that you have stepped into your brother's shoes as it were?"

Jamie cleared his throat and looked lost for a moment. "I haven't had much time to think about it. We are still in mourning…"

"Yes, of course, but surely your father is encouraging you to marry."

"Oh, well he hasn't said much as yet."

"And yet he is certainly thinking it. It is past time, young man. Though of course our own Anne is no fit partner for you, I am sure another young woman can be found in your set."

Jamie frowned and glanced down at Anne for a moment. "Why would Anne not do for me?"

"Really! Her mother's behavior has cast a shadow over her fitness as a bride that no dowry can erase. I am certain your family holds their position far too dear to even think it."

Anne kept her face averted during this exchange, and did not see Jamie's reaction. His cup rattled in its saucer, and his voice had a harsh edge to it when he spoke.

"I hardly see what her mother's actions have to do with Anne;"

"That is a very naïve statement, Lord Ashton. Family missteps are visited upon the young. Evelyn chose to step out from under her husband's protection, and is lost to us now. Half of Anne's lineage is now tainted, and what man will want that taint following his children? No, Anne will do quite well with some lower peer's son who will perhaps be able to overlook her heritage, or at least not berate her for it."

She glanced over. A white dent appeared in Jamie's cheek. Anne frowned at it, only to realize he was angry.

He took a deep breath. "Any man would be proud to call Anne his wife, regardless of what her mother does."

Aunt Gertrude peered at Jamie and her silver eyebrows met in her furrowed brow. She said nothing except to comment upon the poor shape of one of the hedges leading to the house.

Jamie rose up suddenly. "I must return to my father. Lady Anne, would you accompany me to my horse?"

With a glance at her aunt, Anne followed him. As soon as they were out of sight on the front step, he kissed her, soundly, lips seeking hers as he claimed her. Her arms went around him, just as desperate for his touch as he was for hers. They broke away, breathless, to stare at one another.

"Jamie…"

"Anne…" His voice was ragged, and he pulled her close once again. "Marry me."

Her mouth dropped open and she pushed away. "I can't. Please don't ask." She turned away as tears threatened.

He held her back and gripped her shoulders so she could not run.

"Why? Why, damn it?"

"My aunt is right. My mother—"

"Your mother be damned!"

"Don't! Edwin…"

He stopped and straightened. "Edwin. I see." His hand spasmed and then released her. Without looking at her he climbed onto the saddle and galloped off.

She collapsed against the door. Marriage! Oh bliss…but she could not. Aunt Gertrude was right in this. Jamie would see it in time; his father would surely make him see. The Marquess of Marrenfort deserved better…

If only she could convince herself. Almost she called him back, almost she ordered Angel saddled so she could ride after him. But no, she was right in this. She would protect him from himself. She would be strong…

She would die.

After long moments standing on the step, she had some semblance of control and returned to her aunt. Aunt Gertrude had helped herself to another biscuit and looked up with a crumb on her wrinkled lip as Anne walked in. Anne went to her place and picked up her cup without really seeing it. She took a sip and then set it down.

"Lord Ashton has grown into quite the handsome young man."

"Yes," Anne said faintly.

"He needs a wife. He is of an age where a man should take a wife. I am surprised to find him hidden here in the country."

"His injuries."

"Ah, yes. I had forgotten. He seems so fit and hearty one naturally overlooks the fact that he was recently at death's door."

"Aunt Gertrude, would you excuse me for a while? I have a headache and would like to lie down."

"Of course. Take some lavender and put a cool handkerchief over your eyes."

"Yes, ma'am."

Anne left quickly, making her way up the stairs to her room where she fell upon her bed. Why had she mentioned Edwin? She had thought about his secret and how that loomed between them, as well as her aunt's words. Edwin's child. Tell them or not? Surely, she could trust Jamie to know what to do. But how to tell him now?

She curled on her side and crossed her arms in front of her. She needed to find a way to escape from Enniston for a while. To get away from everything she had become entangled within. Her mind went quickly through a very short list of friends and relatives. One name stood out: her cousin Marie de Larrancourt. Distant cousin, it was true, but safe in London and relatively sensible, if something of a flirt. Perhaps she could arrange a visit there to get away from everything for a while.

She made her way to her little writing table and quickly penned a letter to her cousin. Reading it over she thought it sounded slightly desperate, but hoped Marie would not see that. After sealing it, she rang for a maid to collect the note and place it with the rest of the letters to go out.

****

Anne rose the next morning knowing she needed to see Jamie. Somehow they had to communicate and work their way through this. She ate a quick breakfast then dressed in her riding habit to go over and see him.

She was on the point of leaving when Aunt Gertrude arrived.

"Anne, you are dressed to go out."

"Yes, ma'am. A little morning exercise."

"Excellent notion. Stimulating. Then I expect you will practice the harp?"

"Yes of course, if you wish it."

"I do. Safe riding."

Anne went out, grateful to have escaped so quickly. As she came to the path leading to the folly, she turned her to go up toward the lonely little building. Riding up the little track, she turned a corner and found Phaeton, with Jamie seated upon him.

They stared at one another. Jamie looked away first, only to turn back to her.

"Anne…"

"Jamie, you must let me explain."

"Explain what? That you can't marry me for some ridiculous reason?"

The weight of Edwin's secret hovered over her with her aunt's opinions and she hesitated. It was too much, and she found she could not break through the wall they presented. Her hesitation seemed to Jamie to be enough. He quickly turned Phaeton and made to ride off.

"Jamie!"

He paused, but did not look back.

"There are things you don't know. I am just not sure if I can tell you just yet. Please understand."

He inclined his head slightly toward her, then urged Phaeton on and galloped away.

****

Nearly a week passed before Marie's answer came.

Aunt Gertrude had gone, and Jamie had stayed away. The days had been lonely and lackluster as she had stayed away from horseback riding for fear of meeting Jamie out for a ride. As she opened Marie's letter, she held her breath.

Dearest Cousin!

It has been too long, and your letter came at the perfect time! I would love a visit. Things have been so dull around here. Please come as soon as possible and bring your horse. I have been riding lately and you will be so impressed with how well I am doing! Nothing to you, of course, but my riding habit is perfectly delicious! Do write and tell me when you will be here!

Love,

Marie de Larrancourt

Anne breathed a sigh of relief and went in search of her father. She found him in his room going over a ledger and he frowned as he looked up.

"Yes, my dear?"

She held the letter out. "Cousin Marie has invited me to come stay. May I go?"

"What?"

"Marie. Visit. May I?"

"Marie? Oh yes! Yes, of course. Go and have a good time."

"When may I tell her?"

"Any time but next Tuesday. I need the carriage for myself that day."

"Then I could leave Wednesday. It would take two days to get there, so I should arrive late Friday sometime. I shall write her now and tell her."

It was quickly done, and she rang for her maid to tell her the news. Then she went outside to saddle

Angel and ride over to check on Bessie and Elsie.

Her horse had been confined for a few days and was wont to prance with high spirits. Anne let her canter a little to burn off some energy. The countryside slipped by, lit with sunshine from above and various shades of green. They crested the hill and went down the side. After another mile, they turned into the shaded lane and finished up in front of the cottage with its thatched roof.

Anne slid down from Angel's back and went to the door. It burst open. to emit Elsie from her mother's arms, running and laughing. Bessie chased after her.

"Elsie, careful! Lady Anne is here."

"An-An!" Elsie held up her arms.

Anne lifted the little girl up and swung her around, smiling at the child's joyful squeal.

"What is all this?"

Jamie's voice rang out and Anne spun. Elsie waved her hand, then buried her face against Anne's neck. They stared at one another, then Jamie frowned and descended from his horse.

Anne walked calmly toward him and hefted Elsie on her hip. "This is your niece. Edwin's daughter."

Jamie paled, staring at the little girl. Her nose and smile were Edwin's, however, and difficult to argue.

"So that's what… I saw you and followed you to see what you were hiding."

Rage rose up in Anne at the thought that he had spied upon her. "How dare you! You had no right to follow me!" she said in a hushed but angry tone.

Elsie fidgeted and she set her down.

"It…perhaps I…" he faltered, staring at first Elsie, then Bessie, then back to Anne. "I thought…"

"I know what you thought."

Nodding to Bessie, she pulled herself up onto Angel's saddle and rode off, at a fast canter. Tears stung her eyes and she dashed them angrily aside. Following her! Checking up on her activities! How dare he!

Angel seemed to sense her mood and gave a little kick of her hind legs. Anne let her canter on until she slowed to a fast trot. Then she pulled her up to a walk and rode with her head held high. The secret was out now! Jamie knew about Elsie!

What would he do? She was too upset to think clearly about Jamie right now. He had betrayed himself to her, and she would not soon forget it. That he had sneaked along behind her and followed her out of suspicion… No, she would not soon forget that.

Leaning her head back, she closed her eyes. Part of her was relieved that the whole burden of Edwin's secret was now lifted. Jamie knew, and she could trust him to act honorably where Bessie and Elsie were concerned.

Just not where she was concerned.

She counted the days until Wednesday and decided that if she took the carriage now, she could change to the post halfway through and the carriage would be back in time for Tuesday. She rode directly to the stable where she allowed a groom to take control of Angel. Spinning on her heel, she then went into the house to find her father. She rang for her maid and gave quick instructions for immediate packing and then found her father out in the gardens.

"Papa!"

"Anne, look at the improvement in these leaves."

183

Unable to focus on the roses at the moment, she ignored them and simply said, "I need the carriage to take me to the post in Wembley. I want to leave today."

Her father frowned. "I don't see… Why today?"

"Please, Father, may I go?"

He waved her off. "I'll send Elgerson with you as you are changing to the post. Let me go tell him to get ready."

He headed off toward the house and Anne followed him, her anger fading but her resolve still strong. By the time she reached her room she found dresses and petticoats and shifts everywhere as Everly folded and wrapped and swiftly packed the trunks. Anne changed quickly into a dress and pelisse suitable for travelling in and went downstairs to await the carriage.

London called.

Chapter Twenty

Jamie stared at the little girl who had climbed into her mother's arms. Bessie lowered her eyes, and bit her lip. "I'm Bessie, Well, Elizabeth, but everyone calls me Bessie."

"Hello, Bessie. I am Edwin's brother, James. My friends call me Jamie."

"Lord Ashton." She curtseyed a little and swallowed.

"I'm sorry, I had no idea that you or Elsie, existed."

"It was Edwin's idea to keep it all secret for now. We wanted to get married once we found out about Elsie, but the vicar wouldn't do it without Lord Marrenfort's approval and Edwin didn't want to tell him."

"I can imagine. We shall have to tell him, however. He deserves to know about you both."

"Can we wait? I don't know that I am ready to meet Lord Marrenfort just yet."

Jamie crouched down to Elsie's height and regarded her. She edged forward and he held out his arms to her. She shuffled slowly to him, and he lifted her up, ignoring the pain in his chest. This little girl was part of Edwin, and his spirit soared suddenly to think his brother was not entirely gone.

"I'm your Uncle Jamie."

"Jay-me," she said, and he smiled.

"That's right. And you have a grandfather who is going to be so happy to know about you."

"Edwin was afraid…" Bessie said quietly.

"Father has his moments, but this will bring him great joy when you are ready." He set Elsie down and looked at Bessie. "Is there anything you need for now?"

"Elsie's lungs get bad in winter."

"I remember Edwin had a similar problem. Doctor Smythe will set her right."

"Yes, but the fees."

Understanding dawned. "Have him send the bill to me. I will handle it."

"Thank you, sir."

Jamie went to his horse and vaulted aloft. He glanced down at Bessie and tried to smile. "I will wait until you are ready to tell my father, but it should be soon."

She nodded and lifted a hand in farewell. He rode off, his mind awhirl. Edwin a father! And Anne complicit! He had used their "courtship" as a ruse to visit his daughter and her mother. How had Anne felt about that?

He needed to see her, but sensed that she would be too angry just yet. Though he felt some guilt at stalking her that day, he could not regret it. He understood his brother much better now, but was angry at him for keeping the secret so long from their father and him.

Phaeton moved into a fast trot which jarred his chest unbearably. He slowed him to a walk and breathed a little more easily. One thought kept circling his brain. How would he tell his father? It needed to be soon.

Phaeton had taken advantage of his inattention to snatch a bite of leaves from a nearby hedge. He struggled for a moment to focus on the here and now, to get himself and his horse home safely. The day warmed. The shadows shortened, then began to lengthen once more. Marrenfort appeared over the hill, and he let Phaeton break into a canter at the sight.

As soon as the groom took control of Phaeton, he went up to the manor house, hoping to avoid his father. However, the marquess met him coming down the stairs and gave one of his brief, cold smiles.

"Ah, James. Come into my room. I wanted to show you the ledgers."

"Yes, Father."

"If you are up to it, of course."

"I am a bit sore and tired, but I would like to see whatever it is you wish to show me."

"Ah, never mind, then. We can do it another time. Go rest."

"Thank you." He headed up the stairs into his room and sat on the edge of his bed. How was he going to lie to his father now? How had Edwin managed it? For years!

He laid back slowly and inhaled a deep breath. What was Anne doing? Angry at him, still, if he knew Anne. She would not forgive him easily for stalking her. But she would in time. For now, though, he would give her some space while he figured out how to handle his brother's secret.

He dressed for supper and made his appearance in the dining room in time to be seated with his father. It was a quiet affair, neither of them speaking much, though Jamie noted his father had less of an appetite than usual and this fact worried him.

"Father, are you quite well?"

"Indeed, yes. Why?"

"Your appetite."

The marquess put down his fork. "I dislike fish, and yet I know it is a wholesome food. I choked on a bone when I was younger and have remembered it ever since."

Jamie thought back, and was surprised that he had never noticed before. "Why not tell the cook you dislike fish?"

"As I said, it is a wholesome meal that others enjoy. I simply eat more of other dishes when fish is served."

Another instance of his father's sense of fairness and duty that he had never known about. He returned to his meal, his mind putting this piece of information into place. The marquess did the same, picking through the flesh of the fish on his plate as he was wont to do.

Two days passed before Jamie felt ready to attempt to see Anne. He dreaded and yearned for it both at once. He missed her deeply, and yet hated the thought of the argument to come. His heart hammered within him as he rang the bell and waited on the front step.

The door opened and the butler said, "Lord Ashton, welcome."

"Thank you. Can you tell Lady Anne that I am here to see her?"

"Lady Anne is not at home."

"I am sure she instructed you to say that, but could you tell her it is urgent?"

"Sir, Lady Anne left for London two days ago. She is not here."

London?!

"Can you tell me where in London?"

"I believe she is at her cousin's home, de Larrancourt is the name."

"De Larrancourt, in London. Yes, thank you."

He turned in a daze and vaulted into the saddle, spurring Phaeton home. *London? What was she doing in London and why?* The woods sped by as he raced home. Almost he took the short cut over Gypsy's Gate, but at the last minute kept to the drive and went around the long way to the stable.

When he was back in the house, he hunted for his father and found him in his study. Lord Marrenfort looked up in some surprise.

"Father, I need to go to London."

Lord Marrenfort's eyes widened, then his forehead creased, "Why?"

Jamie's mouth fell open and he paused. Sitting slowly in the chair by the desk he glanced at his father. "Anne."

The marquess set his quill down and folded his hands. Then he nodded and said only, "I have to see a doctor in Harley Street. I had planned to leave the day after tomorrow."

"Then, if it is all right, I will join you. I am no less interested in what the doctor has to say."

"I admit it will ease my mind to have you with me. We shall plan to leave in two days. I hope you can wait that long."

"Of course. Thank you, Father."

His desire to see Anne paled next to his father's needs just now. He headed into the hall and down to where the grand staircase met the main floor. He stared around him at the house he would inherit one day and hoped with all his heart it would be a long time hence.

****

The trip to London took place under cloudy skies. Periodic drizzle misted the windows of the carriage, blurring the countryside. His father stayed wrapped in an overcoat, with a rug across his knees. He looked small and almost inconsequential to Jamie who felt suddenly protective toward his father.

The two days to London were long, and it was late when they checked into Mivart's hotel in Mayfair. It felt good to stretch his legs and stand fully upright after days hunched inside a carriage. He paced about his room, seeing to the correct placement of his trunk and bags before heading downstairs to the concierge.

"Please, can you tell me the location of the de Larrancourt home?"

"De Larrancourt? I cannot tell you. However, I will look into it if you wish."

"Yes, please."

Jamie looked around. His father was resting, and it was late enough that he was hungry. He went into the dining room and ate a fine supper before retiring to bed.

The next morning he had breakfast delivered and checked with his father who was seeing the doctor that day.

"Do you want me to go with you?"

The marquess shook his head. "No, son. I would rather hear whatever he has to say alone. You understand, I'm sure."

"Of course, Father."

The door shut softly, and Jamie headed downstairs to the concierge once more. The man recognized him and smiled widely,

"Ah, sir! I have some information for you! The de Larrancourts have a house in Chelsea, near Kings Road."

Jamie grinned in response. "That is excellent news! Thank you," he said as he slipped a coin into the man's hand before going out the front doors in the drizzling gray day to hail a cab.

Chapter Twenty-One

Anne sat listless. Her cousin had been talking for some time about a girl she did not know but who Marie, apparently, disliked.

"And so she danced with him, which vexed me, but she did so poorly that I could hardly keep from laughing. I would not care so much, except that she snubbed me at our first meeting though, after all, she is not so much better than me. Our fathers are both earls."

Anne stifled a yawn and nodded automatically.

"You shall have to come with me to call upon her. You will see what I mean about her figure. Most unfashionable."

"Though she can hardly help that, surely?"

"I should think if my arms were so large I would do something about it."

Anne peered at Marie's rather rounded arms. "But what?"

"I saw a man once, at Vauxhall Gardens. He was lifting great barbells and chairs and people. He had worked his muscles so that they were very large, and it made him quite strong. Surely, then, there would be a way to make one's arms smaller."

Anne was doubtful, but let Marie talk on.

"She does well enough with her gowns, though that is all down to the *modiste*, naturally. You must help me get the name of the woman who does her clothes. I must have her to do mine!"

"I will try to remember."

"Oh, la! How long it seems until there is a ball of any consequence. Isobel Clement is coming out in a few days and mother has secured an invitation for you. She is a little thing—you will not believe how short and thin she is! But I must say she plays rather well and has an angelic voice, as long as you don't notice her collarbones jutting out above her bodice!"

Marie certainly had no need to worry about her collar bones showing, or any bones for that matter. Her plump form sat molded by a corset into conformity and she reached for another chocolate confection on the little table between them.

Marie's voice was pitched just high enough to grate on her nerves, and Anne wished heartily for the quiet of home. She missed Jamie, though she was still angry. *He should have simply come to me and asked!* Perhaps they would be on a different course just now if he had. But then she remembered her mother, and sighed.

"And what was that sigh for? A man I dare say."

"What man would have me, Marie?"

"Oh, we can find you one, don't worry. Unless you have your eye on someone already."

"That's a rather vulgar way to put it."

Marie laughed, then popped a piece of marzipan into her mouth. "There are three or four that I have my eye on. Any one of them can steal me away behind the bougainvillea."

"Marie!" The girl choked as her mother came into the room, picking up sashes and brushes as she went. "Such clutter. What have I told you about talking so?"

"To not to."

"Exactly. Guard your speech as a shepherd guards his flock. Let no untoward euphemisms pass your lips."

Lady Margaret de Larrancourt bustled about, setting things to rights and smoothing her daughter's hair briefly as she passed. Then she was gone, and Marie rolled her eyes.

"Good Lord, Mother!" she said under her breath. Then she brightened. "What luck for you to not have a mother at home."

"Not such good luck, taken all-in-all."

"Mother forbids me to talk about it, but I must own to a great deal of curiosity. How does she live? Does she have regrets?"

"She lives comfortably, though obviously must make do with many things. I think she is happy, she just misses me and is a little lonely."

"I can imagine. Who would call on her?"

"Yes, but she was always a solitary person. She enjoyed reading and knitting, her tambour frame and garden. I don't think she minds it as much as you might."

Marie blew out a long breath. "I should mind it very much. I get so bored, so quickly. Mother says it is because I have such a quick mind, but I think it is just that I am naturally gregarious and prefer to be with people. What about you?"

"I prefer to be around certain people and not that many."

Marie laughed, "Then you won't enjoy Isobel Clement's ball. There will be quite a crush of people there, hardly any room for dancing. You wait and see…"

Anne shuddered a little. "I shall endure it, I suppose."

"Well, what shall we do today?"

"Can we walk to the square? It would be pleasant to be outdoors for a time."

Marie sighed. "I suppose. I had hoped that Lord Standley would call. I want you to see him! He isn't as tall as I would like, but is he handsome! All blond and blue-eyed with just the right amount of color! And his lips... I can tell you I have dreamed about what they might do!"

"Marie!"

"Oh la! As if you don't dream about someone in particular in that way."

"If I do, I don't discuss it."

Marie sat up, her pretty dark head on one side. "And why do we not? Why is it we can't talk about some things? What is so inherently wrong about them?"

"I don't know. Some subjects are just rather unseemly, and some are simply horrid."

"Well, Lord Standley is neither."

"I thought you had a few men you liked."

"Oh, I do. I am not set on any of them. Whichever comes forward first can have me. I am anxious to get away and be mistress of my own place."

"And children?"

"Oh la! I suppose that comes with it. I don't like children as a rule, but I have heard women feel differently about their own. I shall employ a good wet nurse to handle the screaming things and simply kiss them goodnight."

Anne considered such hands-off parenting and it saddened her. Elsie, how happy and warm she was.

Would she would have been nearly so happy living as Marie had just described? She rather thought not.

"I think I will want more input into my children's rearing."

"Better find a man first."

But I have… A little spike of anger pierced her as her mind went to Jamie, and yet she knew that she loved him still. If he asked again, she would accept him, come what may. Time away had taught her that much. Somehow, they needed to break through this terrible curse of miscommunication.

"So, tell me about the new Lord Ashton! His brother's death was a nine days' wonder here!"

"It was rather horrid for us."

"Oh yes, you were there. Did you actually see it happen?"

"I would really rather not discuss it."

Marie sighed. "Fine. Just tell me about Lord Ashton. Is he fearful handsome?"

Was he? It had been so long since she had just accepted Jamie for who he was that she did not know if he was reckoned handsome by most.

"I think so. At least I like his looks," she said.

"What are his looks? I only met him the once years ago when I visited you."

"Well, he is tall, dark brown hair and eyes, high cheekbones…" *Yes, he is handsome…*

"He doesn't sound too bad. Maybe I should visit you and try my hand at him. His father is a marquess, after all."

"They avoid London, however."

"Ah, but that can only last while Parliament is out. Dear Papa must do his duty, and one day the son will

196

take over."

Anne wondered how Jamie would like attending Parliament. He was certainly good at arguing.

The bell rang in the distance and Marie straightened, smoothing her dress and tightening a bow. They sat in silence until a maid arrived to tell them that Lord Standley had arrived. Marie colored and rose, taking the lead before Anne and sweeping down the stairs in a smooth, practiced manner. Anne followed behind her. They went into the drawing room where a young man stood facing away from the fireplace with his arms behind his back. Anne did not think him so terribly handsome, but it was clear that Marie was extremely pleased with him.

"Lord Standley, how lovely to see you."

He bowed over the proffered hand and looked up at Anne, his eyes widening as his mouth dropped open. "I don't believe I have met your guest."

Marie frowned at his expression and shot a glance at Anne.

"This is my cousin, Lady Anne Debenham. She is staying with us for a few days."

He took Anne's hand, bowing long over it. "Enchanted, Lady Anne."

"Thank you, Lord Standley."

Lady Margaret bustled in and the four of them perched on the hard settees and chairs. Anne tried not to look at Lord Standley, but every time her gaze crossed him, he was looking directly at her. Marie's gaze flicked from one to the other and her smile had a hard edge to it.

"Have you been riding lately?" Marie asked.

"Oh, yes. And you? I understand you had taken up

riding."

"I have, and am enjoying it immensely."

"What about you, Lady Anne? Do you ride?"

"Yes, I have always had a horse. Papa insisted."

"There is no felicity like riding through the countryside."

She smiled. "I would have to agree with you there."

Talk faltered then. After a few minutes he rose and thanked them, bidding each of them goodbye, but once again lingering over Anne. As soon as he had gone, Marie turned to her with her mouth twisted down.

"Well, well, well! You seem to have made a conquest."

"Nonsense. I am just something new."

"Indeed. So new and fresh that he could not keep his eyes from you. I see I shall have to be careful who I introduce you to in future."

"Oh, Marie, please don't. His attentions mean nothing to me."

Marie seemed a little mollified by that. She smiled. "Well, you do have the new Lord Ashton to occupy you. How delightful it would be if he happened to call."

"I doubt that; he is in the country recovering from a serious wound."

"What is this?"

"He was shot during a sea battle. He was brought home to convalesce."

"A war hero! Oooh! I must come visit."

The bell rang again, and the three women looked up expectantly. Anne's stomach clenched as Jamie entered.

"Lord Ashton, " the butler announced to a sudden

198

silence.

Jamie scanned the three, but lingered on Anne. Marie preened beneath his brief gaze, but Anne simply met it with wide eyes.

"Jamie, I mean, Lord Ashton. What are you doing here?"

"I am in town with my father. I had heard you were visiting friends and thought I would call."

Lady Margaret smiled and gestured for him to sit on one of the uncomfortable chairs. He chose a spot closest to Anne, though he did not look at her directly.

"This is so unexpected, and yet surprises can be quite nice. How long do you expect to be in town?" Lady Margaret said.

"But a few days, I fear." He turned to Anne, and she read blank accusation in his expression. "And you, Lady Anne, how long do you intend to stay in London?"

Anne cleared her dry throat a little. "A couple of weeks, perhaps. My dates are not yet set."

"I hope we will have you back in west Berkshire soon. You are missed."

His voice turned gentle, and it was as though a knife twisted in her heart as his eyes found hers.

"Thank you. It will not be too long, I think. My father writes to hurry my visit."

"And yet, I don't think I can do without Anne. We have ever so many plans. You should stay longer in London and join us some evening," Marie declared.

"I am at my father's disposal, but thank you for the invitation." Jamie rose and bowed to each of them. "Thank you for the visit. I will try to call again. If you need me, I am staying at Mivart's." With a final lingering glance at Anne, he left.

"Well! I must say I like your lieutenant! Lord Ashton, one day to be Marquess of Marrenfort. Indeed, I like him very much," Marie chirruped, with wide eyes and a smile. "We must have him back. Mother! Mother we must have a musicale and invite his father and him. Can we?"

"Yes, of course my dear. This Friday is free. I shall write the invitations myself. Musicale and a supper, I think."

Anne was silent throughout. Her anger at Jamie had died with that final glance and she felt only the pressure in her chest where she thought her heart might explode. That he had followed her to London, she had no doubt. His actions declared himself, but she dampened her emotion with caution. All she knew for certain was that he was in London, and if Marie had her way they would meet again in a couple of days.

****

The invitation went out and was accepted. Friday came and Anne dressed with more than the usual care. Everly tended to her hair, twisting it loosely into ringlets that fell from a braided bun. Tiny blue silk flowers were woven in amongst them. Anne turned her head this way and that to get a better view. Marie gave her grudging approval, and Anne reached down to twitch her skirt slightly before heading downstairs.

Marie raced her, reaching the ground floor first and leading the way to the drawing room where the guests were already seated. Anne followed more sedately, her nerves a-tingle at the thought of seeing Jamie again.

He stood by the window and turned as they entered the room. His gaze passed over Marie and went straight to Anne. He came forward, nodding to Marie but reaching for Anne. He bent over her hand and looked up at her with his warm brown gaze.

"You look remarkably well, Lady Anne."

"Thank you, Lord Ashton. As do you."

He led her to one of the chairs and seated her. Marie shot her a sullen look, then seated herself on the other side of Jamie. "Lord Ashton, I understand you are recovering from a nasty wound received during a battle. Do tell us about what happened."

"Oh, it was nothing, just a skirmish at sea."

Lord Marrenfort looked at his son with eyebrows elevated. "Do tell us, James. I have not heard the story."

Jamie's eyebrows shot up and he glanced at Anne before beginning. He gave them the bare bones, glossing over his injury but praising Jim for all his care. "Indeed, it is due to him that I am still here. He pulled me to safety and saw me through the worst of the infection that seized me."

"What can account for his attentions?"

"I know the answer to this," said Lord Marrenfort. "Young Mr. Knight relayed to me how James had saved him from going overboard by putting himself in danger to stop him and drag him back. He felt an obligation that needed discharging."

"I am grateful for his friendship, at least."

"I am as well, if it saved you from further injury or death," said Anne softly.

Jamie's gaze shot to her and held hers for a long moment. Marie cleared her throat.

"Yes, we are all glad Lord Ashton is so well recovered. One would never know you had been laid low."

Jamie smiled. "That is the country, I'll wager. Fresh air and wholesome food. And being outdoors as much as possible."

"I understand you ride a great deal," Lady Margaret said.

"Yes, it is one of my favorite activities. Much like Lady Anne. The three of us used to race over the countryside."

"Three of you?" asked Marie.

"My brother Edwin. And us."

A little silence fell, then Marie moved to the pianoforte. She smiled at the company and began a complex Italian song. She played well, with few mistakes, and paused when finished to bask in the abundant appreciation of the little company. Her mother especially applauded her and encouraged her to play again. She chose a German song and played it a trifle pedantically for Anne's taste, but she acknowledged that it was better than she could have done.

It was soon Anne's turn, and she fought the butterflies in her middle. Marie sent her a triumphant smile as she passed by, and Anne's chin rose a little. She sat down and thought for a moment, then played.

It was an old song, but one of her favorites. As she played, she sang as well and knew that she sounded good, if not better than good. Not so complex as Marie's playing, yet it was pleasant and calming. Something Marie's playing had missed. When she finished, there was an outburst of appreciation from the room.

Supper was announced and the company went into the dining room. Anne found herself seated next to Lord Marrenfort and Jamie next to Marie. From the looks Lady Margaret continually threw in their direction, it was not difficult to see the hopes there.

Anne turned to her neighbor. "How are you enjoying your time in London?"

He smiled, hemmed a bit, then said, "I am here to consult with a physician. I am looking forward to going home. London does not suit me."

"I hope the consultation went well. I happen to agree with you about London. I miss my rides over the countryside."

"Yes, I seem to remember you and Edwin used to ride frequently." He seemed a little sad at mention of Edwin but smiled briefly. "You and James used to ride when you were younger. I remember you and your pony on the front lawn, chasing James about with a polo mallet."

She laughed. "I had forgotten that. You're right. I did! Thank goodness I never hit him, though I certainly tried hard enough!"

"You were quite the little horsewoman. James seems to have followed your lead in that. Edwin was not much of a horseman unless it was the hunt." Again, he retreated a little and she scanned her brain to think of something to say.

"I think the gardens at Marrenfort have been looking lovely."

"Yes, we have had good weather for the plants and flowers and such. I must admit to being rather ignorant. I simply instructed the gardeners to carry on with what my late wife had started. I think they may take advantage of my lack of knowledge from time to time."

"I think our gardeners wish Father a little less involved in the roses than he is."

"Ah, but Enniston's roses are famous!"

They were quiet for a while as they focused on eating. Anne could not help but strain to hear what Marie and Jamie might be discussing. She heard Marie's voice frequently, but Jamie seemed limited to very short replies.

She glanced up once to catch Jamie's eye and they shared a look.

Chapter Twenty-Two

Jamie allowed himself the brief pleasure of looking into Anne's eyes. He smiled at her, and she smiled slowly back. Marie continued to chatter,

"And then we danced a third set. You would not believe how the whole room stopped to watch us and even applauded when we were done. My old dance master did say I had a knack for dancing, not that I would ever say so. It's a pity you won't be here long enough to attend the Clements' ball. I am sure we could secure you an invitation."

There was a pause, and Jamie belatedly realized he was expected to answer. "Er...no, I believe our plans are set. We leave in two days' time."

He could hear Anne speaking again and strained to discern what she said. He frowned a little; they seemed to be speaking about horses. What could they have to say about horses?

"And so, we sit for a little in the morning room which has a quite nice view of the street going by. You should call sometime and join us. We would have such a merry time."

"That sounds delightful. I shall have to see if I am at liberty to do so."

"Or, we could take a turn about the block, if there aren't too many carriages and such on the street. I went out for a little fresh air one morning and my frock was ruined by a passing cab."

Jamie said nothing as their plates were taken away and replaced with the main course which seemed to be veal.

"It was one of my favorites, Oh, I wish you could have seen it. White muslin with an embroidered bodice. The neckline was just divine!"

"Er…sounds nice."

"Indeed! But, of course I have many others. Father rather spoils me that way. Anything I want. I am his only little girl, as he says."

Jamie silently sighed as he listened for some sign of what Anne and his father were discussing. Her calm, low voice mentioned Edwin and his attention sharpened. Surely she wasn't telling his father Edwin's secret?

But no, his father was calmly replying something about schools and Jamie relaxed a little. Marie had moved on to another topic.

"Mother and Father insist I go to the country with them every year although I don't see why I couldn't stay in London. Although, I must own that I enjoy the quiet of country life, even though I think there needs to be a few more balls and socials added to improve on the peace and quiet."

"That would rather counteract the peace and quiet."

She swallowed the bite in her mouth. "I suppose, but it needn't be quite so quiet in the country."

Jamie let it go. Anne and his father had fallen silent now, and he wanted nothing more than to catch her eye once more and see that slow smile again. But she was being very attentive to his father, something he could only be grateful for.

Supper finished and they retired to the drawing room again where Marie played once more, and Anne demurred. A pang of disappointment went through him. It was so rare that he experienced Anne's musical abilities, and he had hoped to hear more from her. He realized suddenly that she had many talents he had not yet divined, and hoped again for more time to do so.

Then his father rose and thanked the de Larrancourts for their hospitality. Jamie thought desperately for some way to have Anne to himself, and yet the opportunity was fading fast. As he bent over her hand in farewell, he mouthed, *forgive me?* Her gaze flicked a way for a moment, then returned to his and she nodded. Light and relief shot through him as he straightened, and he knew he was grinning like an idiot by the way one corner of her mouth crooked up. Moments later, however, he was back in his father's carriage with his calm expression.

"I take it this was a successful evening after all?"

"Yes, as much as it could be. She has forgiven me, at least. That is something."

His father nodded and gave a little smile.

Jamie thought suddenly and asked, "What did the doctor say this afternoon?"

The marquess was silent for a moment. "He feels it may not be quite so hopeless, but he has to see me again in a month to check the progression, if any. By then he hopes to see improvement if I follow the treatment prescribed."

"Father, that is excellent news!"

The marquess' expression lightened, and he nodded. "Yes, it has eased my mind somewhat. Still, we must wait another month to see what he says."

That night as he was undressing, Jamie thought over the day and another thrill of hope rang through him. Anne had forgiven him; his father might not be dying. What more could there be?

He fell asleep with his heart light and hopeful.

****

Morning came sullen and dreary. He woke with a headache and lay back against his pillow, groaning. It seemed to happen whenever he came to London. His head would become congested after a couple days and the ache would start. He wondered if it would be too soon to go and visit Anne. Marie had very pointedly invited him to call upon them again. How could he get Anne to himself? First he needed to rid himself of this congestion and pain.

He breathed in some steam with mint leaves and felt his head clear a little. Breakfast helped, as did the coffee he drank instead of tea. It felt robust, and wakened him from his headache in a welcome manner.

"I am meeting with the solicitors today. I think you should join us, Jamie."

Disappointment shot through him, but he schooled his face and nodded. "Of course. I am at your disposal."

"I know you may wish to visit Lady Anne and her delightful cousin again. Perhaps an afternoon call would be acceptable."

His father's eye had a twinkle in it and Jamie smiled a little.

"Yes, Father, perhaps that would do. Thank you."

Jamie dressed with care, and read for a while before the solicitor and his young partner joined them. They spent some time going over accounts and investments, things Jamie had never thought about. He understood why his father had suggested he be present. His head was reeling by the time the two men left the little room where they had been meeting. The marquess then turned to Jamie.

"I am going to lie down for a time. I will not need you again until this evening."

"Then perhaps I will call on Lady Anne and Miss de Larrancourt."

His father smiled and headed up the stairs to his room. Jamie went to the front of the hotel to have a cab called for him, then stepped into the hansom and gave the directions.

The buildings and houses passed by as the cab wove through the carriages and people on horseback. He was always struck with the number of people compressed into such a small space when he came to London or any other city. He could not imagine living like that, and yet life onboard a ship was very similar. Strange, he had never considered life crowded on a ship. Perhaps it was that everyone had a job and worked in a comprehensible manner, whereas the city seemed a chaotic mass of people.

He sighed, leaning forward as the de Larrancourt house came into view. He stepped down and paid the cabbie before heading up the stairs to ring the bell. The butler appeared after a short wait and he was admitted to the drawing room.

Marie rushed in as soon as she saw him and fairly gushed, "Oh, Lord Ashton, so good of you to come again. Come, let's sit in the east sitting room, so much nicer in there. The sun comes in through the trees and it is most pleasant."

Jamie followed her into a long, rather narrow room

filled with portraits and more uncomfortable furniture. He sat on one chair that pressed into the spot on his back where the bullet had lodged.

Leaning forward away from it, he said, "Where is Lady Anne?"

"She was lying down earlier in the day. I shall send a maid to let her know you are here. The city seems to have that effect on some people." She made no move to do so, however.

"I woke with a headache this morning. I know how that feels. Are you sure we should not send someone to Lady Anne now?"

After a moment, Marie went to the bell and instructed the servant who came to call Anne. It was some time before she came downstairs. She sat down equal distance from Jamie and Marie, but smiled upon Jamie.

"I would never have thought you would heal so quickly. It is good to see you up and about so much. I pray you do not overdo it, however."

"I am doing my best to be careful, I assure you."

"So dreadful, getting shot! And I think I heard something about you having another adventure to do with a ship...?"

The old fear rose in him, and he battled it down. Anne reached for him, then pulled back as though suddenly mindful of Marie's presence. The walls shook as the cannon balls hit, the floor exploding out from under his feet...

He covered his face with his hand and swallowed. "The French ship shot at us, and their ball went through the ship and hit the powder kegs. They ignited and blew... I was tossed into the sea with a few others who quickly succumbed. I held onto decking as the ship went down with the rest of the crew. There was only me left when the *Tempest* arrived."

The room was silent.

Marie's mouth lay open as she stared at him. Finally she said, "It sounds terrible. How horrible for you to go through. Thank God for the other ship!"

"Yes, I do so every day."

"It's a miracle you were not injured," Anne said.

"Yes, battered and bruised was all. Nothing to speak of."

"And so you have resigned your commission?" Marie asked.

He hesitated. "I have not, as yet. I am torn."

"But surely you are needed at home…"

"And yet, the country needs me as well. I don't know what to do. I am almost well enough to return."

"But…you can't!" she insisted.

"Jamie must do what he feels is right, in this as in all things," Anne stared at him.

"I'm glad you see it as I do. The case is not so clear as Miss de Larrancourt might like."

Her eyebrows were up and her eyes wide. "I should think it was clear to anyone who knew of your story. Let others fight. You are needed at home. Who will inherit if you are lost?"

"Who indeed? But if England is lost…?"

"Surely there is no fear of that?"

"If everyone felt as you do, it may come to that."

They were silent.

Marie took a breath. "Well, enough of this dreadful topic. Let us have some tea, shall we?" She got up to ring the bell and as soon as the servant arrived, ordered that tea be brought in. Then she sat and smiled at Jamie. "So, Lord Ashton. Can you not be persuaded to stay for the Clements' ball?"

"When is it?"

"Friday."

"I think that is the day we are leaving."

"But think, if you stay just another day or two, what fun it would be."

He was tempted. The thought of dancing with Anne was intoxicating. He tilted his head slightly. "Perhaps, if an invitation could be secured for me."

Marie bounced and clapped her hands. "Oh, I shall have Mother write the Clements today and inquire. It will already be a terrible crush; what will one more body be?"

Jamie stood, thanking her and with a final look at Anne, left to return to his father. The more he thought about it, the more he wanted to stay for the ball, if only for a chance to be with Anne for a few moments.

He found the marquess in one of the common rooms, discussing the current political climate.

His father turned to him rather testily. "Yes, James?"

"Father, an opportunity to attend a ball has arisen. Would it be possible to stay in London another day or two?"

The lines on the marquess's forehead deepened. "I can't think of any reason why not. Though, I wish I could. Still, there are things I can do here if we extend our stay."

Relief rushed through Jamie, surprising him. He had not known how much he had looked forward to possibly dancing with Anne. Nodding to the other inhabitants, he backed away and went to the writing desk to pen a note to the de Larrancourts accepting their invitation, should it be extended to him.

Then he smiled to himself.

Chapter Twenty-Three

Anne stood staring at the image in the mirror. Her maid had done her hair beautifully, in curls that cascaded from a twisted bun. Her dress was the lavender silk with the intricate braid around the neckline and Van Dyke points on the sleeves. She wore simple pearls and gold earrings and hoped Jamie would like the overall effect.

The carriage swept them across Chelsea to the Clement home. A large townhome in a fashionable area, it looked broad and well-maintained. Judging by the line of carriages, there would be quite a few people within.

Minutes passed as they waited to get nearer to the home. Marie stared out the window, squeaking with excitement when she saw someone she recognized. By the time they were released from the carriage to go up the short walk, Anne's stomach turned over and she did not trust herself to speak.

As Marie had predicted, there was a terrible crush inside. People were pressed together. Music played from the ball room and Marie pushed to get them through the throng to where the dancing was. Her hand gripped Anne's tightly as she pulled her between bodies until they reached the floor where they pushed forward to watch the dancing.

Having little experience of large balls, Anne was

quite overwhelmed. Awe struck her at the mass of colors and fabrics all mingling and circling. Suddenly her view was obscured, and she glanced up to see Lord Standley there.

"Lady Anne, may I persuade you to dance?"

"I-I, why yes," she said as her mind blanked on how to get out of it.

His elbow thrust toward her. With a glance at Marie, who had flushed an unpleasant shade, she laid a hand on it. Anne swallowed and allowed herself to be drawn out onto the floor.

She quickly took stock of the dance and their place in it. Then they were off. Lord Standley danced well, and Anne worked hard to remember the steps and keep herself in the right space. She tried not to look at Marie, but her gaze was drawn to her cousin. She was dismayed to see her still standing there, her face schooled to a mask of indifference.

Sighing, she took his hand, to be spun about and came face to face with Jamie!

He reached for her and they stepped off, Lord Standley forgotten. Jamie's hands upon her, light but sure, moved with her rather than forcing her. They turned, changed partners, came back together, and the dance ended.

They stared at one another. Then he guided her gently back to where Lady Margaret and Marie waited. Lord Standley was nowhere to be seen.

"You are not with the man you left with," Marie said.

"No. I seem to have exchanged partners."

"That is quite—"

"Miss de Larrancourt, would you dance next with

me?"

Marie's eyebrows rose. "Why yes, Lord Ashton. Thank you."

Jamie shot a glance at Anne as he took Marie to the dance floor.

Anne was almost as happy to simply see Jamie as to dance with him. He moved well, despite some stiffness to his shoulders. She frowned a little at this, knowing he must be in pain despite the sanguine expression.

She stood in the shadows, as Marie and Jamie waltzed by, with a twinge of jealousy that she wasn't in his arms instead. But his gaze turned to her continuously, and she knew he felt the same. By the time the dance was over, Marie puffed from the exertion and Jamie breathed with some difficulty.

Fanning herself, Marie sat down, with her mother at her side. Anne led Jamie to a chair beside the windows and bid him sit. He slowly lowered himself, wincing, and she bent forward solicitously. He grabbed her hand and pulled her closer, staring into her eyes. Her heart pounded as she lost herself in the brown depths of his eyes.

"Anne..." His gaze dropped to her lips.

She glanced to the side where people stood. He leaned back slightly.

"What can I get you for your relief?"

He winced and straightened, "There is nothing, I just need to rest a while."

"Dancing is far more energetic than it looks."

"It is, and I have never been much of a dancer."

"I thought you did quite well!"

He laughed shortly. "Then you weren't watching

very closely."

"I can assure you I was."

Their gazes met once more, and the room around them faded. Anne stood on his right side, protecting him from the crush of bodies around them. Her hand rested on his shoulder, one finger stroking his neck.

His shoulders stiffened, then his hand gently covered hers for a mere second, before returning to his lap. After a few minutes his breathing eased, and he led her back to where Lady Margaret sat.

"Oh! Marie is off dancing. You can see her there. Lord Standley asked her. They do make a fine couple, do they not?"

"Indeed, they do," said Jamie. "I am going to escort Lady Anne to get some punch. Can I get anything for you?"

"I thank you, but no. I have partaken of the refreshments already, and I wish only to watch my girl dance."

They left her then, weaving through the crowd to where the punch table sat amidst the sandwiches and confections. Both helped themselves and retired to a pair of open seats at the table. It was as if lightning had struck her, enlivening every part of her being.

Then something grew in her mind, a heaviness as she thought of Bessie and Elsie, the burden that Edwin had left with her. The marquess needed to be told, before anything else could be settled. She needed to put this connection with Edwin to rest.

"Jamie."

He turned to her, his face very near to hers. They stared at one another for a moment, then she murmured, "We need to tell your father about Edwin. I can't go further until that is done."

He looked at her for a long moment. "We should do it together. When will you be home?"

"I can leave anytime as long as Lady Margaret sends a man with me. I will let you know as soon as I arrive."

He nodded, his gaze flicking over her face. Then he helped her to her feet. "I'm about done for. I shall return to the hotel so that Father and I can leave for home tomorrow."

"I'll let them know that I will be leaving in a few days. It will take that long to arrange everything."

They parted, and Anne made her way slowly back to Lady Margaret. Marie was gone, out on the dance floor somewhere and Anne stood, relieved. She watched the dancing for a time, joining in occasionally so as not to elicit any comment.

Marie returned, her bosom heaving from exertion. Her curls were beginning to droop from perspiring and she fanned herself assiduously.

"Oh, Lord! Such fun. Anne, you aren't dancing."

"No, I enjoy watching, though."

"She danced once or twice after Lord Ashton left."

"Lord Ashton left?"

"He was tired. His wounds made it difficult to continue."

"Oh yes. He is a good dancer. Perhaps not as good as Lord Standley, but I enjoyed my dance with him immensely."

"Well, my dear. It seems to be time we were leaving."

Marie pouted, but the crowd had thinned considerably. Lady Margaret led the way for them to claim their wraps and they waited as their carriage was fetched. The night air puffed before the horses' faces and wreathed them in a smoky aureole as they strolled down to the waiting carriage. The streets were nearly empty, and a drifting fog flowed about in a ghostly manner.

They arrived at the de Larrancourt home as the clock in the hallway rang the fourth hour. Anne made her way to her room and was met by her maid, who yawned before undoing her dress and helping to take down her hair. Finally, she was snuggled under the covers and fell asleep before the door shut.

****

The curtain rings rattled gently and sunlight streamed in. Everly set the tray on the table beside the bed and Anne groaned, pushing the ruffle of her bonnet out of her face and sitting up. Her head felt thick, and she rubbed her eyes as she looked around.

"What time is it?"

"Past one, m'lady."

"Mmmph. And is that tea?"

"Yes, m'lady."

Anne pulled the tray toward her and poured a cup. She took a long draught and sighed. She had work to do today. Somehow, she needed to arrange her return to Enniston, and Jamie. She nibbled the toast Everly had brought and dressed in her pink-sprigged muslin dress. Everly arranged her hair and then she went downstairs in search of Lady Margaret.

Silence reigned on the main floor, letting her know that neither Marie nor her mother were awake. She wandered into the smaller sitting room and sat beside the window, watching people and carriages pass by.

The clock had struck three before Lady Margaret appeared. She draped herself over the chaise and heaved a heavy sigh. "Goodness, I used to dance the night away and be up before the next morning had gone. Now, I can barely stir myself before supper."

"I think Marie is still asleep."

"I heard her maid taking a tray in to her. Lord Standley was very attentive last night."

Anne smiled, but said nothing. After a little silence, she said, "Lady Margaret, I feel it is time for me to return home. Would it be possible for you to send a servant with me?"

"What? Leave us? No! I'm sure Marie would be heartbroken."

"Nevertheless, I feel I must go. My father misses me and hurried me home in his last letter." Anne uttered the lie with a straight face and only the tiniest twitch of her nose.

"Well, my dear. I think we can arrange to send old McMurtry with you. He can't do much these days except keep the kitchen fire stocked. When did you wish to go?"

"However soon it can be arranged."

Lady Margaret was quick to organize it, and Anne went in search of her maid to let her know. As she climbed up the stairs, she met Marie who rubbed her eye and yawned.

"Hello, cousin."

"Marie."

"Where are you off to?"

"I am leaving in another day or so. I need to tell my maid."

"I see. Perhaps it is for the best. I am expecting

Lord Standley to make his proposal soon, and you tend to distract him." She looked quite keenly at Anne.

Anne nodded, and after a moment, Marie smiled and continued on her way. Anne found Everly who simply began to sort through her clothes. She hummed a little, which let Anne know that she was quite happy to be leaving.

"What shall you wear on the way home?"

"I think the muslin with the rose buds and my pelisse. The matching bonnet, of course."

Everly set the items aside so as not to pack them. Anne stood beside the window, looking out. Now she was anxious to get home, and the time could not go by fast enough.

****

Four days later she stepped from the carriage and trotted up to the front door of Enniston. She was struck by the smell, a mixture of polish and wood and herbs. It was the smell of home and she breathed it in with a smile. Her father wandered out of the library and saw her, his mustache tipping up in the corners as he made his way toward her and pulled her close.

"Ah! My girl is home! All is as it should be."

She grinned at him and untied her bonnet, then let it drop beside her as she held the ribbons.

"I must change, and a bath would be heavenly."

Everly went by her carrying a pair of hatboxes. "I've already arranged it, m'lady."

Anne followed her maid up the stairs to her room where the tub was being wheeled. The fire had taken the edge off the room. Can after can of heated water was brought in and poured into the tub. Then she stripped down and stepped in, hastening to wash so she could get out and dry off before dressing in clean, warmed clothes.

She shivered as she sat before the fire, warming herself and waiting for the gong to ring. When it sounded, she scurried downstairs to the dining room where her father stood waiting for her. They sat and the footmen began serving the meal.

Her father smiled frequently. "And how are our cousins, the de Larrancourts?"

"Quite well, Father. Marie may be getting engaged soon."

"Indeed? Well, well. Now we just need to get you engaged."

She smiled and looked down at her plate.

A footman brought her a note and said, "The boy is waiting, hoping for a reply."

Anne read the short missive and nodded. "Tell him yes."

"What is it, Anne?".

"Just a message from Jamie. He wants to take me out in the barouche tomorrow."

"Ah. What fun. Just like old times with Edwin, eh?"

"Yes, Father."

She struggled to keep her heart from beating so wildly and took several steadying breaths in between the courses. She hardly knew what she ate, only that the next day she would see Jamie and they would begin working through this mess they were in.

****

Morning brought a flurry of nerves as she went through her routines, just waiting for two o'clock when Jamie's note had said they would call. She stood on the front step as the barouche trundled up the drive with Jamie at the reins. He jumped down to help her up and she nodded to the marquess, bundled up in rugs and scarves against the cool spring air.

"I don't know what all the secrecy is about," he said.

"We will find out soon enough," she replied.

The trip took a while as the barouche was a little slower than plain horseback. By the time they pulled up in front of the thatched cottage, the marquess frowned at it and looked around.. Jamie helped them both down and the door opened.

Bessie emerged, holding Elsie's hand.

Elsie waved a plump hand, then pulled free. "An-An!"

Anne scooped her up and nuzzled her, then turned to Lord Marrenfort. Jamie stepped closer.

"This is Edwin's daughter. Your grandchild."

The marquess's eyes widened at Elsie. She stared back, Edwin's parentage written in her expression when she smiled at him. Lord Marrenfort looked from one to the other, then his gaze gravitated back to Elsie.

"But I thought you and Edwin…"

"He loved Bessie and wanted to marry her. I was simply complicit in the secret."

The marquess looked at Bessie who straightened a lock and twitched her skirt a little. She bit her lip uncertainly as she stared back with her lovely eyes. He reached out a hand to her and she held hers out to him.

"My dear, I am very glad to make your acquaintance."

She curtseyed. "The honor is mine, Lord Marrenfort."

He turned back to Elsie, wonder mirrored in his eyes as he gazed at the little girl. Hesitantly, he held his arms out to her and she leaned closer to Anne for a moment, then slowly reached for her grandfather who gently took her. He hefted her securely as tears glistened.

"What a miracle child you are, little Elsie. A miracle indeed."

Jamie nodded to Anne. "It is all on her. She discovered Edwin's secret and provided a cover for him. She encouraged him to tell you, but he kept putting it off. We felt it was time you knew."

"Yes, yes indeed I should think it was." His voice cracked and Elsie wriggled to get down. His gaze followed her as she ran to her mother and swung from her arm, and he smiled. "We shall have to have you up to the house soon. I should like to get to know you both better."

Bessie nodded, appearing too overwhelmed to speak. Slowly the company returned to the barouche and the marquess stared at the little pair in front of the cottage until they were out of sight. When they had turned onto the main road, he dug a handkerchief out to wipe his eyes and blow his nose.

"Excuse me, Lady Anne."

"Not needed, sir."

"I thank you for all you have done for our family. I hope your connection to us remains strong."

"I hope so as well."

When they reached Enniston, Jamie jumped down to help her out of the barouche. He walked her to the door., "I should like to call on you tomorrow. Perhaps we could ride together."

"I should like that."

His hand pressed hers, then he let go and went back to the barouche and his father.

She watched until they had disappeared into the woods before going into the house.

Chapter Twenty-Four

Jamie felt his father's gaze upon him as they drove, but maintained his control of the horses. He dreaded the scene when they reached the manor. What was his father's reaction going to be once away from innocent eyes?

He dropped his father off at the front of the house, then took the barouche back to its spot beside the stable. With a deep breath, he headed back to the manor and the confrontation with his father.

The hall was empty when he went inside. But light came from the open door of his father's room and he headed there after a moment's hesitation. He found his father seated at his desk, staring at the papers before him, though obviously seeing none of them. He looked up as Jamie entered.

"I have misjudged you most of your life, and said some unforgivable things to you. I would beg your forgiveness for this."

"Father…"

"No, I am serious. You reminded me of my father who I disliked, and I have punished you for another man's transgressions long enough. I own to have been wrong, and sincerely ask for your indulgence."

"Father, it is yours."

The marquess nodded. "As for little Elsie, I will of course support her in your brother's name. She will have some inheritance from me. It is just for me to decide what." He paused then added, "She has a look of your brother about her. Her smile…"

"Yes, with her mother's eyes."

"Indeed. I look forward to improving my acquaintance with her. This has come as a shock, but, I believe, a welcome one. It feels right, somehow, that there is something of Edwin alive still."

"Yes, Father. I feel the same."

He left the marquess in his room and headed back out into the cold main hall. The candles had not yet been lit, though twilight had descended, and shadows filled the space. He moved through the gloom until he came to the drawing room and stood looking over it, remembering the many times Anne had sat within, laughing, talking, playing.

Anne.

He glanced through the tall windows at the darkness growing. A maid came by to shut the curtains and he went to his room to change for supper. Lightness trickled through him, and uncertainty. He felt he had done his duty by his brother; now it was time to do the same for himself.

Tomorrow.

His father was quiet throughout supper, and he sat just as silent, though it was a comfortable space that night. There was much to think of, and no need for words between them.

****

Jamie woke late the next morning. He stretched, his body alive and awake, ready for what needed to be done. He dressed, ate breakfast, then rushed out to the stable to collect Phaeton. The sun had risen. It warmed the air and melted the frost sparkling over the damp grass and leaves.

Phaeton stepped lightly, seeming to float and bounce with energy. Jamie rode down the drive toward the woods, passing Gypsy's Gate. A bird settled on the branch, then flew into the air to soar high overhead. Jamie watched it for a moment, then continued on.

It was early, so he rode to the folly, only to find Angel grazing there, her reins dragging on the ground. He slipped down, glancing round for Anne, knowing she must be close.

"Anne?"

"Here," she called out from behind the Athena statue.

He went to her and pulled her close, then tilted her head up to his and lowered his lips to hers. She pressed against him, arms snaking around to his shoulder. They stayed lost to each other, until Angel nickered and they broke apart.

"Marry me," Anne said.

"Yes," Jamie answered, then smiled down at her.

She sighed, closed her eyes, and leaned against his chest. His arms rose to hold her securely to him.

They savored the silence. After a time, he kissed her again, long and slow. His body stirred and his heart raced with excitement. She was his!

"We need to tell our parents," she said.

"We will." With a sigh, he pulled back, one hand tracing her cheek and down to her neck before dropping away. "All right, then, let's tell them. I'm sure we'll end up at the same house sometime today."

"I need to tell my mother."

He nodded. "Which shall you do first?"

"Mother, I think. Father is with his steward now and would not like being interrupted, however wonderful the news."

He kissed her again. "The let me go tell my father. I love you."

"I love you, oh, how very much."

He grinned. "As you should!"

Before she could react, he bounded up onto Phaeton and rode away. He pushed his horse to a canter as they made their way down the path to the little road through the woods. His heart pounded in his chest and he breathed deeply, ignoring the stabs of residual pain.

The woods were coming to an end. He turned to go up the drive toward the house, gaze on the distant stable, mind on how he would tell his father this latest news. Suddenly, a pheasant burst out from under the cover, flying up into Phaeton's face.

The horse jumped to one side. Jamie caught sight of one wild eye as Phaeton reared and charged away from the bird's flapping wings. Jamie nearly fell off as he jolted to one side, but clung with his legs to the saddle and the stirrups. He pulled back on the reins but Phaeton did not respond and galloped wildly through the bracken.

Gypsy's Gate neared. He hauled on the reins to turn his horse. But hooves pounded inexorably for the dip of the stream before the gate, muscles bunching as he flew to clear it.

Phaeton rose, but not high enough. His hind leg caught on the trunk and pulled him down, throwing Jamie over the horse's head.

Chapter Twenty-Five

Anne rode to the house at the very western end of Brumley. She found her mother scouring a pan. Evelyn's eyes widened as she took in her daughter and pulled her quickly into the house.

"My dear, what is it? You look so alive!"

"I am! Oh, Mother..." She hugged her tightly and whispered, "I think I begin to understand." She glanced over the interior of the cottage with a new sight, taking in the gentle presence of her mother and the calm, happy demeanor of her being.

"Oh, my dear. I am so glad. But what has happened?"

"It is Jamie and me. We are getting married!"

Another hug, her mother pressing her close and bursting into tears. "It is as I had always hoped. My misstep has not injured you."

"No. You have nothing to berate yourself with."

"Not so long as you are happy!"

"I am! Oh, Mother, I am!" Anne kissed her, then pushed away. "But I need to go tell Father. He doesn't know yet."

With a laugh, Evelyn gave her a little shove. "Then go tell him. He will be happy as well."

With a gay wave at her mother, Anne turned Angel around and rode off. She loped gently along, rocking in rhythm with her horse. She came to the branch in the road and started to turn toward Enniston, but a movement stopped her. Anne frowned, for there was nothing there. But she reined Angel to a stop as she stared at the spot she had seen move.

Slowly she edged Angel toward it. They came to the little rise, where one could look down through Gypsy's Gate to Marrenfort. Something fluttered in the breeze and she peered closer, only to cry out and urge Angel forward.

Anne slid down and ran past Phaeton who stood off to one side with one leg raised. Jamie lay sprawled in a heap on the far side of the gate, and she rushed blindly forward.

His eyes were closed. She bent over him to listen to his chest but her own heartbeat pounded in her ears, and she could hear nothing. She licked her lips and held them close to his, finally feeling the cooling of his breath. He was alive! But how to get him to safety?

She looped Angel's reins under his arms and secured them there.. Anne urged her forward and slowly, step by step, they pulled him up the rise until he lay on the top of the hill, near where he had sat in his invalid chair not too many weeks ago.

She removed her jacket and laid it over him for added warmth, then raced off on Angel's back to find some help. She rode first to the stables where she informed the grooms of what had happened. They instantly hitched up the cart to retrieve Jamie. Then she rode to the house where she did not wait for the butler, simply let herself in and stood in the main hall calling, "Lord Marrenfort! Sir!"

A door opened down the passage and the marquess emerged frowning in confusion. Suddenly his air changed and he rushed forward.

"Where is James?"

"Injured. I found him at Gypsy's Gate. The grooms are going to get him."

"Take me to him." He called the butler and directed him to send a message to Doctor Smythe, then followed Anne outside.

Together they raced off down the rise toward the slight crest where Jamie lay. The grooms emerged from the stables with the cart and hurried forward to check on Jamie. His father knelt down, as did Anne. He bent and listened at his chest, then looked up as the cart neared them. It took all of them to lift Jamie's body and place it gently in the bed of the cart. Then they headed slowly back to the house.

It took nearly an hour to get him there and up into his bed. Anne hovered beside him, listening desperately for the doctor.

Doctor Smythe finally arrived and shooed everyone from the room. Anne stood with Lord Marrenfort in the hallway, who paced up and down. Half an hour later the doctor emerged and called to Lord Marrenfort, who nodded at Anne to follow. They went to the bedside.

Jamie's eyes were open, though bruised. His gaze went from one to the other. "Did you tell him?"

Fighting tears, she shook her head and he reached weakly for her hand. "Anne and I are getting married."

Lord Marrenfort's eyes misted over, and it took him a moment before he could speak. "You have no idea how happy this makes me. But son, why did you jump that infernal gate?"

"Bird flew up at Phaeton's head. He shied. I

couldn't turn him."

"I will have the thing burned. Immediately." He turned to the doctor. "Will he be all right?"

"He's broken a collarbone and cracked some ribs, but he should be fine." He looked at Jamie and smiled, "You're going to get a reputation as being immune to death."

"He won't have the opportunity to test it. He's staying home, aren't you, son?"

Jamie glanced at Anne and nodded. "Yes, Father, I'm staying home."

Anne gripped his hand and smiled as they stared deep into one another's eyes. Lord Marrenfort cleared his throat and left the room.

"I really have you..." he said.

"Yes, it's always been you, Jamie."

He smiled. "I rather like the sound of that!"

She rolled her eyes then traced some scratches on his face. "You must stop these brushes with death, though."

He nodded. "I've been a sight too lucky. I'm keeping my feet on the ground from here on out." His brow creased. "I can still ride horses, though, can't I?"

Then he laughed and she bent to kiss him.

Epilogue

Anne rose up before her maid had a chance to rattle the curtain rings. Her trunks were packed; her wedding dress lay pressed and ready for her to don. The night before she had bathed and washed her hair. Everly was already getting the table ready to brush out the long plaits and dress them.

She ate the toast and eggs that her maid had brought, and drank the tea in a few gulps. Then she was sitting at the table, staring into the mirror with wide eyes as her maid worked her magic.

As she watched herself transform from young lady into a bride, she thought about the real transformation that would take place when she became a wife. Her heart pattered wildly, but she was ready for it and embraced the idea with open arms.

Her father was quiet as they entered the carriage and rode down the drive toward the Brumley church.

"Are you well, Papa?"

"Oh, yes, indeed. Going to miss you a bit."

"I shall be next door. You will probably see me just as much as you do now."

"Well, my dear, I certainly hope that is so."

The carriage rolled up before the church, but they had to wait as another discharged its passengers. Anne peered out the window, hoping to catch a glimpse of her mother who had promised to be there.

Then her father helped her down himself and led her through the arched doorway and down the aisle. Her mother sat toward the back with Havers, who smiled at her. She smiled back, then looked toward the altar where Jamie waited.

Scarcely hearing the vicar, she held tightly to her flowers and tried to focus on speaking at the correct time. Jamie slipped a ring onto her finger and she said something in response to the vicar, but her gaze had met his and she had gotten lost once more. They were announced and she faced the crowd of people filling the church as Jamie's lady, his wife.

The wedding breakfast was long, and by the time the guests left Marrenfort, Anne was all but exhausted. Jamie, too, though recovered, found he was ready for the last of the guests to go. Except for Jim, who had come back to stand with Jamie on this day and was a guest at Marrenfort.

Finally, the last guest was gone.

"Well, my lord. Will you show me to my quarters?"

One corner of Jamie's mouth quirked up and he bent to kiss her. "That I will, my lady."

A word about the author...

As long as I can remember I have been writing and making up stories. After moving to Georgia in 2002, I became busy as a foster mom and department chair at a community college and writing kinda fell off the map for a while even though my husband kept at me to keep writing. I also pursued my love of fiber arts (using a spinning wheel to make yarn from wool and other fiber) and so the phrase "spinning a yarn" has a double meaning for me.

Enter my daughter, Crystal who is also a writer. She was determined to get me writing again and in August of 2019 presented me with several romances and informed me that I had six weeks to write a book to pitch at the upcoming Moonlight and Magnolias writing conference in October. So, I wrote one. Then another. Then I finished writing a couple novels that had been sitting around for years. Now I am back to working at getting my novels published.

My husband and I have adopted three children, and I am now an online professor, leaving me lots of time for writing. I write just about every day, and spinning seems to help the muse along.

****

https://gracecolline.com

****

If you enjoyed this story, leaving a review at your favorite book retailer or reader website would be much appreciated. Thank you!

www.ingramcontent.com/pod-product-compliance
Lightning Source LLC
Chambersburg PA
CBHW051639260626
47170CB00004B/1242